AMERICA CALLING 911

Vincent Armstrong

America Calling 911
Magic Rainbow
Copyright © 2017 Vincent Armstrong

ISBN: 978-0-9853029-9-3

Cover illustration by Suzannah Safi
Formatting by Polgarus Studio

Chapter 1

It was a beautiful Saturday, the first of October, as the clock struck noon. Suddenly, the fuse to a stick of dynamite was lit as unthinkable acts of terror and violence began to happen simultaneously around the country.

On a downtown street in Chicago, the Black Unity Coalition, a national activist organization that protested injustices against African Americans, held a huge rally to protest the recent police killing of an unarmed black man. Hundreds packed the middle of the downtown street protesting when masked men suddenly crashed the protest and started firing semi-automatic assault rifles into the crowd.

Chaos quickly ensued as people ran and screamed. Dozens of bodies, torn apart by flying bullets, began dropping in the street three and four at a time. The pain and agony on the faces of the unsuspecting people were nothing but sheer terror. People desperately tried to escape the blood, gore, and carnage while being mercilessly trampled over.

At the same time, at an atheist march held in Washington D.C., hundreds swelled Pennsylvania Avenue marching with huge banners that read GOD DOESN'T EXIST and RELIGION IS DEAD. Suddenly, live hand grenades from an unidentified source were tossed into the crowd of marchers. Explosions ripped like a butcher's knife into the flesh of numerous marchers as bodies began dropping like dead horses. Utter madness and pandemonium quickly erupted. Survivors ran for their lives as the White House, in the far background, gleamed like a beautiful monument.

As the lit fuse to the stick of dynamite curled quickly like a snake, in Seattle at the Freelife Wellness Abortion Clinic, the place was packed. Women steadily entered the establishment for their assigned appointment times to get their abortions. Some women seemed nervous and uneasy while they waited in the crowded reception area to be called to the back to get their procedures underway; others appeared calm and composed as if they'd been down this tenuous road before.

While the Freelife Wellness Abortion Clinic was busier than a beehive, a young lady, who appeared nervous, entered the packed establishment and stepped to the receptionist desk to give her name for her appointment. Soon as she gave her name and was told to have a seat, a bomb suddenly exploded as everyone inside the place was instantly killed. Simultaneously, the same horrific explosions began happening in abortion clinics in Denver, Sacramento, Portland, Phoenix, and Atlanta.

As abortion clinics exploded in cities across America, at the Islamic Brotherhood Unity Mosque in Manhattan, NY, the mosque and its members prepared for service in observance of the holy month of Ramadan. The Imam began reading to his members from the Quran when a bomb suddenly exploded killing everyone inside. At the same time, another mosque in Brooklyn unexpectedly exploded, while two mosques in Boston were simultaneously bombed and destroyed.

The fiery lit fuse continued to sizzle and snake closer to the dynamite while these deadly coordinated attacks had the entire nation in a state of shock. Police departments in cities across the country, the Federal Bureau of Investigation, and the Department of Homeland Security quickly began to investigate what transpired. News agencies, straining to find out the cause and reason behind the unspeakable tragedy, began to get leads from different sources as they tried to puzzle together what happened.

Finally as evening fell over the nation and no confirmed answers as to who was responsible for this unspeakable tragedy surfaced, panic began to grip the entire nation. People appeared to fear America was under a deadly terror threat it hadn't experienced in years. As a result, stores and restaurants closed early. Ballgames were terminated. Parties and celebrations everywhere were canceled. The streets and highways across the country literally became vacated as people fled from potential danger and locked themselves in their homes.

While the minutes continued to tick late into the evening, tension gripped the nation even tighter. The mounting fear were as if the nuclear button itself were about to be pushed. The intensity kept building. The fuse sizzled. Fear and stress escalated. The terror around the nation had gotten so intense and the pressure had become so great until the dreaded dynamite finally went boom!

Chapter 2

Joshua Edwards was literally glued to his TV in his Los Angeles bedroom. For five hours straight, he hadn't taken his eyes away from the TV screen. He'd been watching the urgent breaking news reports, constantly flipping the channels on his remote back and forth to all the cable news network stations. With his laptop in his lap as he sat in his favorite reclining chair, he tried to figure out what he would write for his blog concerning the tragedies that had just exploded across the country.

His blog, Justice For All, was a social commentary on the state of America's problems and issues concerning poverty, race, culture, religion, crime, the judicial system, politics, and many other social issues that affected the everyday man. It was a blog that he put out weekly, followed by over two million faithful followers each week. The fact that his blog ranked as one of the most read blogs in the country each week, and the fact that he was the only African American blogger in the entire country who commanded such prestige, made him extremely proud.

While Joshua stared at the breaking news that continually came across his TV screen, he had yet to write a single word to his weekly blog. For five straight hours, his mind had literally been dumbfounded and rendered incapable to come up with anything to say. Not only had the horrendous events of the day stifled his mental ability to focus on what he needed to say, but the fact that he terribly worried about his son's condition certainly wasn't helping.

His twenty-three-year-old son, Kahila, was a member of the Los Angeles branch of the national organization Black Unity Coalition. Kahila, along with the entire branch from Los Angeles, had gone yesterday to Chicago to take part in today's huge protest.

The ongoing situation in Chicago had Joshua unnerved and on edge. Not knowing the condition of his son, and unable to reach him on his cellphone, had him dreading the worst. He couldn't even get any information when he tried over and over to contact the numerous hospitals in Chicago to see if his son had been admitted because of the mass shooting.

Joshua knew his twenty-three-year-old son, at six-foot-three weighing two hundred forty pounds, could certainly take care of himself in a crisis, but not against a mass, murderous shooting. Every time the house phone would ring and each time his personal cellphone would go off, Joshua hoped and prayed that it would be Kahila calling to tell his father and mother he was okay.

Of the countless calls that continued to bombard the house, none, however, were from Kahila. A persistent array of calls from all sorts of friends and associates who wanted to talk about the deadly attacks that the news endlessly reported kept coming one after another. Joshua, though, had enough. The only call he wanted to hear from next was his son.

When Joshua suddenly heard his wife pull into the driveway with her car and park, he quickly turned down the sound on the TV in the bedroom. He had yet to talk to his wife on the phone since the tragedies first began happening around noon, but he knew full well that she'd probably already heard every news report and detail by now. The fact that he hadn't been able to get in contact with Kahila or find out any information from any of the hospitals in Chicago made his stomach turn.

On the other hand, his twenty-one-year-old daughter, Tyesha, on an overnight trip to Las Vegas, had called a few hours earlier, so he already knew that she was okay. Kahila's current state of condition, however, was another story. Because of this uncertainty, Joshua almost dreaded looking into his wife's eyes. He truly dreaded having the conversation with her about their son when she finally walked into their bedroom.

Joshua didn't have to wait long for his wife's presence. When she entered the house, she quickly came storming up the winding staircase of their beautiful two story home like a track star trying to break a world record.

The pain on his wife's face when she stepped into the bedroom was clear evidence that she'd already heard the devastating news. Joshua's beautiful wife of forty-six all of a sudden looked twenty years older. The worry lines around her forehead and the way her cheeks sagged in the center of her face, made her almost look like a crack addict who'd come running to a crack house to score another bag of dope. Her eyes had a skittish, nervous glare that looked like death had encroached upon her. Joshua almost didn't recognize his beautiful wife of twenty-five years standing in the doorway of their bedroom. She had an ominous, foreboding look that made the unsettling feeling in his stomach grow even worse.

"Have you heard from Kahila?" she quickly asked with desperation in her voice.

"No, I haven't," Joshua said with trepidation. He slowly got up from his reclining chair and began to pace around the bedroom. "I've tried to call his cellphone several times, but I haven't been able to reach him."

While Joshua paced around the room, his wife, Faye, slowly walked toward their widescreen TV in their bedroom and began to stare at the news anchors who commented about the attacks. The sound was on mute, but the way she had her eyes focused and fixated on the TV screen, the sound might as well been on full blast.

"When did you hear about the attacks?" Joshua asked in a solemn voice as he continued pacing.

"About an hour ago when I finally got out of that long meeting we were having downtown at the headquarters of A Hand In Need."

"Have y'all been meeting this entire time?"

"Yeah." Faye slowly nodded as she continued to stare at the TV screen. "We were organizing this fundraiser for the underprivileged children here in Los Angeles and discussing the upcoming national convention next month in New York. We were trying to coordinate all of our upcoming events with all the other chapters in the other cities, when someone suddenly looked at their smartphone and saw what was going on."

"What was the reaction when everyone found out what was going on?"

"All the ladies in the room were in total shock," Faye said, suddenly grimacing when the news showed a replay of all the injured marchers in Washington D.C. lying bloody in the street after the hand grenades were thrown. "I actually didn't know about the shooting in Chicago until I was coming home and heard it on the radio."

"You didn't know about the shooting in Chicago?"

"No." Faye slowly shook her head, still grimacing. "The ladies at the meeting only mentioned what was happening in Washington D.C., the explosions at those abortion clinics, and those mosques being bombed. They didn't mention a thing to me about the shooting in Chicago at the Black Unity Coalition protest march."

"They probably didn't want to alarm you, Faye."

"Have you tried contacting any of the hospitals in Chicago?" she said in an almost petrified voice as she turned from the TV screen.

"I've tried calling every hospital in Chicago for the past two hours, but nobody seems to have any information."

"Well, we need to catch the first flight out of here and head to Chicago," she said in a panic voice. "We just can't sit around here and be totally in the dark about Kahila's condition."

"Faye, it's already after five p.m. here in L.A., which means it's seven o'clock Chicago time," he said as he suddenly stopped pacing and looked at his wife. "We might not get a flight out of here until first thing in the morning."

"I don't care what time it is!" she yelled as her eyes shot like fire. "We need to get a flight to Chicago, and I mean right now."

"Faye, let's just calm down and be a little patient," he said in a composed voice. "I'm sure Kahila is alright. I think the hospitals would've contacted us by now if something had happened. I'm sure Kahila will probably call before the night ends."

Faye glared at Joshua for a long second as if she wanted to pursue the conversation further, but instead, she slowly turned and once again watched the silent TV screen.

"Well, have you heard from Tyesha?"

"Yeah. She called a couple hours ago from Las Vegas. She said she's fine and she should be back in L.A. some time tomorrow."

"I didn't know Tyesha was going to Vegas," Faye said with concern as she turned and looked at Joshua. "Who did she go to Las Vegas with?"

Joshua slowly let out a long sigh as he began to rub his temples. "She said her friend, Patricia."

"Good lord," Faye said as her eyes narrowed while she glared at Joshua. "I hope she didn't go to Las Vegas for no damn quicky marriage or something. Is she *seriously* going to go through with marrying that girl like she's been promising and proclaiming that she's going to do for the last couple of months?"

"I don't know, Faye," Joshua said with a deep sigh. "I can only hope that she doesn't. But if she does, I think it would be her way of somehow getting back at us."

"I'm totally against that!" Faye said with rage as she suddenly pointed her finger. "Totally!"

"Well, so am I. But it ain't nothing we can do it about, now is it? I mean, after all, she's a grown woman now. She's twenty-one with a mind of her own."

"We didn't raise her to be that way," she said in a steamed voice. "I can't even bear to think of Tyesha even contemplating marrying that white girl."

"Would it make any difference to you if she were black, yellow, or blue for that matter?"

"Don't get sassy with me," Faye yelled. "I blame this all on you and that blog you've been writing these last couple of years. You've been promoting the virtues of homosexuality and lesbian issues in that blog of yours for so long, that it's rubbed off on your own daughter, which is the reason why Tyesha now wants to marry a damn woman."

"I don't promote any virtues of homosexuality or any sort of merits of the pleasures of being a lesbian in my blog," Joshua said heatedly. "I merely state that the LGBT community shouldn't be discriminated against or treated with bias when it comes to the rights that we all live by. But I certainly don't promote any virtues of homosexuality in my blog."

"Sure you don't," Faye said sarcastically.

"No, I don't!" Joshua said with fire. "Now if you're that upset with the way that Tyesha has chosen to express her sexuality, then maybe you need to look in the mirror. Because isn't it the mother's responsibility to raise her own daughter the way she would want her daughter to become?"

"How dare you—"

The house phone suddenly rang as Joshua quickly dashed to the nightstand to answer it. Hoping that it was Kahila finally calling, he immediately began to groan when he saw on the caller ID that it was his brother, Conrad.

"Yeah?" he said with a snap when he picked up the receiver.

"Josh, my producer and I want you on the radio show Monday for the whole two hours of the show," his brother said in a hurried voice. "We got a lot to discuss. This stuff that's been going on around the country today is turning out to be the hottest topic of the year. So get your game ready for Monday, little bro, and come on."

"Look, Conrad, Faye and I are waiting for Kahila to call as we speak. He went with the Los Angeles branch of the Black Unity Coalition to Chicago for that big protest march that they were having today. We're a little worried if he's alright."

"I understand. But I need an answer if you're coming on the show Monday?"

Joshua suddenly gripped the phone tighter and glared at the receiver. He couldn't believe the lack of compassion and empathy that his brother showed him, but knowing how obnoxious his brother could be at times, he really wasn't all that surprised.

"Look, Conrad, Faye and I are really stressed at the moment," he said in a terse voice. "I'll call you tomorrow and we'll discuss this matter further."

"No can do, little brother. My producer needs an answer tonight."

Joshua gripped the phone so tight, he literally thought he would crush it into a million pieces. "Well, I guess you'll know your damn answer if I show up Monday, won't you?"

He slammed the phone down and stared at it as he silently cursed his brother. When he began to collect himself, he slowly turned and looked at Faye. The argument they had before the phone rang had now seemed to fade away. He looked into her eyes and could sense the worry, apprehension, and concern that she had for Kahila, had once again returned.

"Look, Faye, let's try not to worry. I'm sure Kahila—"

No sooner than he began to speak, the phone suddenly began to ring once again. This time it was his cellphone. Joshua quickly went across the room to the reclining chair where he'd left his cellphone and grabbed it. He immediately recognized the number on the caller ID and quickly answered his phone.

"Hello."

"Dad—"

"Kahila!" Joshua said with relief as his wife quickly rushed to his side to hear the conversation. "Are you alright?"

"Yeah, I'm alright," he said in his deep voice. "Me and a couple of others just got released from a hospital here in Chicago for minor injuries. But all in all, I'm alright."

"I've been trying to get in contact with you since the reports came over the news about the shooting. I was worried something terrible had happened."

"Well, I got a few nicks and bruises when the shooting started and everybody started running for cover. It was over five thousand of us out there, and it was pure chaos," he said as he suddenly hesitated. "When those masked men dressed in all black, whoever the hell they were, started firing into our crowd, a couple of us immediately got knocked hard to the ground. I believe that's what really saved us. Those of us who got knocked to ground got saved, because the people who were running for cover got sprayed by the bullets. Folks were being rushed to the hospital for bullet wounds and all kind of cuts and bruises. You name it."

"The news said that eight people in Chicago were killed."

"Yeah, little Demetrius Turner, from our branch of the Black Unity Coalition in L.A. who made the trip with us, was one of them. And the bad thing about it, little Demy had been my homie since the sixth grade," he said in a sad, sullen voice. "It's just a messed up day, man. A messed up day."

"When are you coming home, Kahila?" Faye asked with concern in her voice as she suddenly got in on the conversation.

"We're staying overnight, Mom, then we'll be getting on the buses tomorrow morning and heading back. Of course, the people who have more serious injuries and those who are in critical condition certainly won't be getting on the buses and making the ride back tomorrow."

"How many in your group from L.A. are in critical condition?" Joshua asked as he took control of the conversation once again.

"There are two in our group in critical condition," Kahila said with remorse. "Of course, there are other members from other branches of the Black Unity Coalition from other cities in bad shape, too."

"Well, I'm certainly glad that you're alright, son, and I'm glad you're safe," Joshua said in a pained voice. "And I hope you know that I love you."

A long pause suddenly engulfed their conversation as they went silent. The silence seemed like an eternity.

"I got to go. I'm out," Kahila finally said in a clipped voice and hung up.

When Joshua finally set his cellphone down after the conversation with his son, he could still hear the aloofness and detachment in Kahila's voice when he told him that he loved him. He knew that he and his son, over the years, had never had the best relationship.

With their deepest worries of the moment now seeming to be over, Joshua slowly grabbed the remote to the TV and once again turned up the sound. He and Faye slowly sat on the edge of their bed as they continued to watch the news coverage on the TV.

Finally, by the end of the night, the news reported that one lone organization began to take credit and full responsibility for the tragedy that had transpired. A white supremacy and anti-government extremist group called Purification Of America Today, that went by the acronym P.O.A.T., emerged as the lone suspects that had inflicted this grave coordinated attack.

It was midnight as Joshua sat alone in his study on his computer searching the Internet. Knowing he'd be discussing the severity of the tragic incidents that happened around the country today in his weekly blog in a few days, Joshua searched for information concerning the hate group, Purification Of America Today, that had claimed responsibility for the attacks. He'd found their website and was scanning all the vicious, hateful rhetoric that they spewed over their site.

What he read literally horrified and appalled him down to his inner soul. The deep hate and utter loathing they had for African Americans, Hispanics, Jews, Muslims, gays, and other minorities and controversial issues pertaining to America were disturbing and repulsive. Joshua slowly read the mission statement that Purification Of America Today had posted on their website. It was a creed that each member of their organization had sworn an oath to:

The mission of Purification Of America Today is to rid America of the corrupt, deviant culture that has manifested itself over all fifty states of this country and that has corroded the sacred values that this great nation once stood for. We no longer accept nor adhere to the open door philosophy of the great melting pot which has now tarnished the purity of this once great land.

Furthermore, we firmly and wholeheartedly, in this twenty-first century, promote the cleansing and eradicating of this new mongrel race mixing, the ideology of equality for all, and the distribution of our country's wealth and resources to an

undeserving minority class that's ever growing. We will do
everything in our power to bring back the values and principles
that this nation once stood for.

On our dying breaths of every one of our brethren, we will
restore to the white race the power and the dignity that we so
richly deserve, so that we may live in peace and harmony in the
land that God preordained for us.

After reading the mission statement that the white extremist hate group, Purification Of America Today, had posted on their website, Joshua leaned back in his computer chair as he contemplated how he would address today's tragedy in his weekly blog. He knew, whatever he wrote, that over two million faithful followers would be swayed one way or another by his mere words.

Joshua started his blog, Justice For All, ten years ago as a venue to express his views and feelings on social issues that had struck a chord deep within him. After spending nearly fifteen years writing as a journalist for major newspapers in Washington D.C., Boston, Philadelphia, and New York, Joshua yearned to express his views on issues ranging from crime, race, religion, and culture without being hampered by editorial constraints that the newspapers he worked for through the years had placed on him.

In an ironic way, Joshua got his wish when he found himself without a job ten years ago when newspapers across America began to slowly downsize because of declining circulation numbers. This paved the way for Joshua to pursue his journalistic ambitions in a totally different form.

When Joshua was let go from the *Washington Star*, the last newspaper he worked as a journalist for, he and his family returned to Los Angeles, the city where Joshua grew up, as he began working at various jobs to make ends meet while he started his blog, Justice For

All. After a few years of slow growth as he began to attract followers to his powerful, progressive blog, he soon began to catch fire. Within five years, he had over a million faithful followers to his weekly blog and it continued to grow.

The rewards and perks to his growing successful blog soon provided for an affluent life for Joshua and his family. Companies, mostly African American businesses and corporations that wanted to advertise their products to an ever growing base of followers on his rising blog, soon began calling.

Joshua's strong, powerful message grew even more in demand as he began to supplement his wealth of ideas and thoughts with numerous well-crafted books that he commenced writing. Books on the topic of social issues affecting not only African Americans, but American society as a whole, were written and published.

Titles like *The Lunacy of The Second Amendment in the 21st Century, Examining The Hip Hop Culture in Today's Politics, Is Prison Ensnarling Our Black Youth?,* and *America's Third World Public Education System* soon became popular books. Joshua quickly caught the attention of the media with his bestselling books as he became in demand for guest spots on various talk shows across the nation; he also became a hot item on the lecture circuit. Within ten years of writing his immensely popular blog, Joshua, at age forty-seven, had written seventeen books in which seven had made the bestsellers list.

Tired of contemplating what to put into his blog for the week concerning the attacks, Joshua finally closed out of the hate group's website as he turned off the computer and headed out of the study. He climbed the winding staircase of their beautiful multi-million dollar home and headed for bed.

When Joshua entered the bedroom, he saw his wife, Faye, already asleep in bed. The night lamp still burned on the nightstand on his side of the bed as he quickly changed out of his clothes and put on his pajamas. Before climbing into bed, Joshua couldn't help but take a long, hard look at his sleeping wife as he smiled to himself.

Joshua was not only proud of his wife, but thankful to have her. He and his wife had endured a rocky relationship through many years of their marriage. Things had only gotten better between them within the last couple of years, and Joshua knew the reason for it.

Faye, a college-educated social worker who worked for years dealing with the endless issues that many big city social welfare programs often presented, had left her job ten years ago and had formed her own organization called A Hand In Need. A Hand In Need, which had grown over the years and now had regional chapters in twenty cities across the nation, was a nonprofit organization that raised money from donors across the country to help those who were homeless, who needed clothing, and who needed housing. Her job as head executive of the twenty chapters of A Hand In Need kept Faye quite busy and away often as she traveled from city to city to conduct business.

The time away from home and away from one another, ironically, was the antidote that had seemed to heal the deep problems that Joshua and Faye had with one another over the years. Now they were in love more than ever, and it didn't seem as if anything could tear them apart. Whenever tensions did rise between them or would get hot, usually time away from one another would soothe whatever troubled them.

As Joshua began to climb into bed, his cellphone suddenly rang. For the life of him, he couldn't figure out who could be calling at such a late hour. He dearly hoped there wasn't anything wrong with his son, who was still in Chicago with the Black Unity Coalition or his daughter who'd gone to Las Vegas with her friend.

Not wanting the unexpected phone call to wake his sleeping wife, Joshua hurried and grabbed his cellphone from the nightstand next to his bed. He quickly glanced at the caller ID on the phone to see the identity of the caller, but the only thing the caller ID said was unavailable.

"Hello?"

"Mr. Joshua Edwards?"

"Yes, who is this?"

There was a long pause. "This is George Washington," the caller finally said in an old raspy voice.

Joshua pulled the cellphone from his face and glared at it for a second, not knowing what to make of the caller. "Who is this and want do you want?"

"This is George Washington," the old raspy voice said as he paused once again, "and I'm a member of the great organization Purification Of America Today."

Joshua slowly pulled his cellphone from his ear and glared at it once again. "Is this some kind of prank call?" he said as he gripped his phone. "How did you get this number?"

"Oh, this is not a prank call, Mr. Edwards," the voice said in a cryptic tone. "For the next several weeks, you and I are going to become pretty close."

Joshua slowly gazed at his wife, snuggled underneath the covers of the bed, and saw that she still slept peacefully. He could feel his heart beginning to beat faster as he gazed around the bedroom. It took a couple of seconds before he could finally respond.

"Why . . ." he said in a nervous voice. He had to pause and clear his voice. "Sir, why are you calling me?"

"I've read your blog many times, Mr. Edwards, and you're one of the reasons why America must go through a purification. You're the reason why this country must go through a deep cleansing of its soul because of liberals like you."

"I don't understand."

"Oh, you will, Mr. Edwards," the caller said in a cryptic voice. "You will."

The caller suddenly hung up. Joshua stared at his cellphone for the longest when the conversation had ended, not knowing what to make of the strange, mysterious call.

Chapter 3

Monday afternoon Joshua headed to Sunset Boulevard to the radio station Sunset 101. The radio station was a local talk radio show that discussed the latest issues of the day as listeners called in to give their opinions on the various subjects of discussions. It was a talk radio station hosted by Conrad Edwards, Joshua's older brother. Every so often, especially when the issues of the day were hot, Conrad and his manager would ask Joshua to come on the show to discuss the important topics of the day.

Joshua had a somewhat strained relationship with his older brother. Conrad, at age fifty, was three years old than Joshua, and growing up, he always wanted to be the domineering big brother who wanted his little brother to follow in his footsteps. Instead of being the little servile kid to his older brother, Joshua, however, grew up contesting and competing with his older brother in every facet of life.

Whatever Conrad did or grew to like as a youngster, Joshua would do the same, only he would outshine his older brother by a mile.

Conrad played football all four years in high school, finally got to start on the varsity his senior year, and ended up just an average lineman who had to go to junior college to further his football ambitions as a walk on. Joshua played basketball and started three years on the varsity in high school, made all city his final two years, and got a full four year scholarship to play college ball at Stanford. Conrad barely got accepted at a Division III college after playing two years at junior college. He also had to work a forty hour job to pay his college tuition, and he barely finished with a 2.8 grade point average; Joshua got a free ride all four years of college and finished with a 3.7 grade point average. Conrad majored in journalism, finished college, and for years, struggled to find employment at several low paying small radio stations; Joshua finished college with a journalism degree and immediately started working for some of the biggest newspapers on the East Coast.

Not only did Joshua outshine his older brother when they set foot in the corporate world, but now Joshua had seven national bestselling books under his belt. He also had a blog with two million faithful followers that made Conrad burn with envy.

When Joshua arrived in the parking lot of Sunset 101, he parked his car and immediately entered the building. Joshua knew he was heading into hostile territory today when he stepped to the receptionist desk to inform the employee of his arrival.

Sunset 101 had a conservative format with listeners that supported their programming, and with Joshua having a somewhat liberal stance, his views were usually in the minority. Whenever Joshua was invited to come onto the radio show to debate the latest issues, he always felt like a man at a carnival sitting in a dunk tank waiting for all the radio callers and listeners to hurl their questions at him. Joshua knew that his brother only wanted him to come on the radio show today so that his callers would get under his skin with their unrelenting, tough questions. With all the incendiary events that had just happened across the country in the past forty-eight hours, Joshua had fully prepared himself today to get soaking wet.

After Joshua had checked in with the receptionist, a staffer at the radio station promptly escorted him to the control room. When they reached the control room, the staffer politely opened the double glass doors as Joshua entered the room.

Conrad, the host of the two o'clock daily show promptly named Talk Back Today, was already sitting in a chair at the audio control console with his headphones on preparing for the upcoming show. Joshua slowly strolled to the control console as Conrad, without looking up from his work, merely pointed to an empty swivel chair next to him as Joshua had a seat.

For nearly ten minutes, Conrad busied himself with all sorts of papers and notes and flipping switches endlessly on the audio control panel as he never once looked up and greeted Joshua. Joshua merely looked at his brother with a slight smirk as Conrad went through all the bluster of busying himself.

Joshua knew his brother, who at six-foot-five weighing nearly three hundred pounds who towered over his younger brother by five inches and a hundred pounds, wanted to appear important in front of his younger, slimmer brother. Every time Joshua came on the show, it was the exact same routine; Conrad was much too busy before the beginning of the show to say even a word to his brother. Joshua couldn't help but chuckle as he watched his busy brother at work. After all these years, he knew that Conrad still wanted to seem as though he was more dominant and more important than his younger brother.

When two o'clock struck and a red light in the control room lit up, the studio engineer gave Conrad the signal to begin the show. Joshua quickly put on his headphones and pulled up to his microphone as Conrad pulled up to his. It was show time. Talk Back Today was now on the air.

"Good afternoon, Los Angeles, on this beautiful Monday afternoon. It's 2 p.m. on the West Coast, and now it's time for another round of the show Talk Back Today," Conrad said as he started the show in his usual rich baritone radio voice. "Today we're going to be talking about the tragic incidents that happened all over the country this past Saturday that rocked our nation, and we have with us to discuss the subject of today my brother, Joshua Edwards, the esteemed author of the blog Justice For All."

After getting the show started and discussing a few preliminary issues concerning the attacks with Joshua, Conrad began to open up the phone lines and take calls from the radio listeners.

"Hello, you're on the air here at Talk Back Today. What would you like to add to the subject concerning the devastating attacks that happened Saturday?"

"What happened this past Saturday in our country was a travesty, and it totally goes against our country's spirit of life, liberty, and the pursuit of happiness," the caller said in a determined voice. "But the way this country has been going down the wrong path for so many years, it has emboldened radical extremists to take measures into their own hands to rectify the grave problems that our country is going through. And I truly believe, Mr. Joshua Edwards, that liberal voices like yours have helped to fuel the radicals in this country to take unwarranted extremes to do this."

"I totally reject that insane, ludicrous notion," Joshua said heatedly. "What happened this past Saturday across the country was nothing but a murderous rampage by an evil extremist organization that perpetrated their hatred and violence on the American citizens. No opinionated voice, whether it be liberal or conservative, should evoke in someone the kind of carnage that this hate group, Purification Of America Today, inflicted on the people of America. That was just evil at its pure utter worst, and to suggest that anyone's point of view is the cause of such a travesty is a travesty in itself."

When the call ended, Conrad took another caller from the switchboard.

"Next caller, you're on the air here at Talk Back Today. What is your comment or question concerning what has taken place over the weekend?"

"I want to ask Mr. Joshua Edwards does he believe in God?" the female caller asked.

Joshua slowly turned and glanced at Conrad in the studio as Conrad merely looked at his brother in silence. When the unwanted dead air began to intrude upon the show, Conrad gave Joshua a hand signal to keep the conversation going.

"Yes, I believe in God," Joshua finally answered. "In fact, I'm a devout Christian."

"Then why do you fully support and take the stand in your blog for the Pro Choice movement? The sacredness of life, even in the unborn, is a God-given right to everyone. If you and others like you would only see that, our country would no longer need the plethora of abortion clinics that populate the landscape of our country."

"Are you in any way suggesting that the coordinated bombings that happened this Saturday to the abortion clinics in Denver, Sacramento, Portland, Phoenix, and Atlanta were due to my position on abortions in this country?"

"No, not directly. But people like you who have the mouthpiece to advocate for abortion rights give indirect influence for abortion clinics to flourish all around this country."

"I totally disagree with that assumption, ma'am," Joshua said to the point. "And I don't appreciate being implicated in any sort of way as a co-conspirator in these evil, dastardly attacks that have rocked our nation."

When the call ended, Conrad took the next caller from the switchboard.

"Hello, and welcome to Talk Back Today," Conrad said as he greeted the caller warmly. "What is your comment or question concerning the attacks that occurred this Saturday?"

"Mr. Joshua Edwards, your position on gun control has been pretty harsh over the years," the male caller said as he jumped right in. "You've pretty much denounced the second amendment entirely on your blog several times and have even written a bestselling book *The Lunacy of The Second Amendment in the 21st Century* which chastises American citizens of their freedom and right to protect themselves. Why do you promote such an un-American view?"

"If you've followed my blog and read my book *The Lunacy of The Second Amendment in the 21st Century,* I do not propose to eliminate American citizens of their right to own a handgun. But there needs to be a major overhaul to this amendment to not allow for access to these semi-automatic weapons that have no use being in the hands of ordinary everyday citizens.

"A well regulated militia doesn't mean that a housewife in Utah should be able to get her hands on something that can blow a hole through a vault at Fort Knox or shoot a hundred rounds in ten seconds flat," he said with intensity.

"So, you're not proposing to do away with the second amendment?"

"No, I'm not," Joshua quickly answered. "However, there needs to be an adjustment to this amendment, and the quicker we as everyday citizens and our elected representatives see this, the better off we as a nation and as a society will be. If these evil men of this wretched, malicious organization called Purification Of America Today hadn't been able to get their hands on the assault weapons that were used to commit the deadly killing spree that they imposed on so many innocent victims, maybe the death toll from Saturday's massacre wouldn't be so drastic as it turned out to be."

"But don't you believe that if some of those people at that rally in Washington D.C. and that protest march in Chicago would've been armed with whatever weapon of their choice, they could've properly defended themselves and lives could've been saved?"

"Sir, that's merely a hypothetical assumption. Only the complete ban of all assault weapons is more of a certainty that mass killings can be prevented."

"You and fellow liberal blowhards like you are not going to create a socialist state out of this great country of ours," the agitated caller said. "The second amendment gives every American the right to protect themselves, and it's not going to change."

When the caller hung up, Conrad went back to the switchboard and took the next caller in line.

"Welcome to Talk Back Today. What is your comment or question concerning the attacks that happened this past Saturday?"

"I want to say what happened to this country this Saturday was horrible and downright despicable, and I want to totally agree with Mr. Joshua Edwards that his beliefs should no way be construed as any sort of reasons why these attacks occurred," a gentleman caller said. "But, Conrad, I want to ask your brother a question concerning the protest march that the Black Unity Coalition organization held in Chicago this past Saturday to protest police brutality against blacks that has been reported going on there. Do you also believe, Mr. Joshua Edwards, that the Black Unity Coalition organization should also protest the widespread black on black shootings and other crimes there in Chicago that are reported to be one of the highest in the country? Isn't that just as important?"

"I've been a major proponent from the very beginning of ending not only black on black crime in America, but white on white crime, Hispanic on Hispanic crime, black on white crime, white on black crime, Asian on white crime, or any race, for that matter, that commits crime," Joshua said in a strong voice. "But to sit here and suggest that police brutality against blacks in America doesn't exist and shouldn't be brought out to light would be a terrible misgiving on my part.

"The Black Unity Coalition has done a valuable service of not only pointing out the grave disparities inflicted upon fellow African Americans in this country when it comes to injustice, but they must continue pointing out those injustices to make America a balanced and fair union not only for African Americans, but so that every disadvantaged minority group in this country can live without the specter of racial profiling constantly staring them in the face and disrupting their lives."

"Yes, I agree. But don't you think their efforts would be far more beneficial at trying to reduce the rampant black on black crime that exists in many of our cities?"

"You're suggesting that African Americans in our inner cities are committing rampant crimes, but there are no hard facts or substantial statistics or quantitative data that supports your claim. Crime is committed by a wide range of individuals in our nation's cities that has nothing to do with the color of one's race."

"The number of arrests and the conviction rate of African Americans in some of our largest cities seem like hard core proof to support my claim."

"And, sir, that's another whole story altogether of the unbalanced, prejudicial nature of our judicial system in our country that will take literally hours to try to sort out."

As the show went on, Conrad continued to take question after question from callers that bombarded the radio station with their mixed views and opinions concerning the shocking, disturbing attacks that had the country in an uproar. The questions and opinions were unrelenting. They kept coming as fast as machine gun fire, and they were all directed at today's guest, the esteemed Joshua Edwards.

When the show finally ended two hours later, Joshua was as exhausted as if he'd just run in the Boston Marathon. He slowly slid off his headphones and glared at his brother. Conrad, busy shuffling away papers from the show, still wasn't talking. Joshua, however, had had enough of his silence. He was now ready for a little brother to brother sparring.

"Thanks a lot for coming to my defense during the show," he said with malice. "You hardly said five damn words the whole two hours."

"Hey, you're the big time blogger and bestselling author around here," Conrad said in jest as he continued putting away papers. "I thought you had the stomach for a little hard boiled debate."

"You know what I mean!" Joshua said with a snap. "Hell, you usually add a little commentary here and there to gloss over some of the rough spots whenever they arise when I come on the show. But today you hardly said a word. I literally faced a lynch mob today, and if I didn't know any better, I'd say you had this planned all along."

"Maybe I did." Conrad suddenly chuckled as he finally glanced at Joshua. "Don't be so upset, little bro. You handled it fairly well."

Joshua glared at his brother with an even nastier look than before. "Don't expect me to do you any favors anymore," he said as he leaned in Conrad's direction. "You hear that—*big bro?*"

With a quick whirl, Joshua suddenly rose out of his swivel chair and stormed out of the control room.

After leaving Sunset 101, Joshua headed to a small rib joint that he frequented from time to time in the Crenshaw district before he decided to head home. He needed a place to unwind after spending two straight hours being grilled about his political views and debating issues nonstop.

There was no place better to unwind than Sam's Rib Shack, where black people of the streets told things like they were. Joshua may have had a big house inside a gated community in an upscale neighborhood, but he still kept his connections with the everyday people whom he loved to associate with. They kept things real, and Joshua wanted to remain real no matter the level of success that he attained.

Joshua entered Sam's Rib Shack when he arrived and headed straight for the bar. The place, small and quaint, was sparsely filled today with a few regulars as they sat around eating and having light conversations. Seventies R&B music played on the restaurant speakers, and there was a widescreen TV in the corner of the place on mute as it showed ESPN.

Sam's Rib Shack was a neighborhood joint that was a mixture of half restaurant and half bar. It was run by Sam Shell, a former NFL player in his late sixties who was built like a huge grizzly bear. Sam, whom everyone simply referred to as Big Sam, had a friendly disposition to just about everyone who ventured through the doors of his establishment. He could make a depressed soul feel as high as a mountain before that person departed his place; but even more important, Big Sam, without a doubt, served the best ribs west of the Mississippi.

"My main man, Josh," Big Sam said from behind the bar with a hearty smile when Joshua had a seat at the bar. "What you having today? A slab of ribs with a tall bottle of beer?"

"Big Sam, you know I've sworn off drinking for the last ten years," Joshua said with a laugh. "No, I'm not that hungry. Just bring me a mess of hot wings and a Coke."

Big Sam put in his order for hot wings and filled a large glass with ice and Coke as he served Joshua his soft drink.

"I just got through listening to you on Sunset 101 not long ago in the office back there," Big Sam said with a smile as he hovered near the bar. "Those callers were nailing you to the wall today."

"That's putting it mildly," Joshua said as he grabbed his glass and sipped his Coke. "I was more like run over and stampeded by an endless pack of angry conservative dinosaurs as huge as those in Jurassic World.

And my wonderful brother Conrad virtually stood by and let all of it happen. That's the last damn time I'll make myself the scapegoat for his listeners on his radio show just to help him out."

"Your brother still jealous of you?"

"Always has been. He never could stand the fact that I could even come close to doing anything better than he could. It's been like that for years. Now it just eats at his soul and pride like some kind of cancer that's slowly killing him."

"So, it's like a constant competition thing with you two?"

"More like with him. He feels like he has to be my competitor in whatever we do. I got a good job right out of college as a journalist with a big newspaper in New York, so he tries to get on with the top radio news conglomerate in the country. I become successful nationwide with my blog, so he tries to get his own national TV talk show and become a big time talking head. I grew up with somewhat liberal views, so he becomes conservative, and so forth."

Joshua's hot wings were finally ready as Big Sam placed his order in front of him.

"So, what do you make of all these attacks that happened this past Saturday?"

Joshua shrugged as he bit into a hot wing. "It's crazy. I've never seen anything like it."

"I know your son, Kahila, is a member of the Black Unity Coalition. Didn't he go with the branch out here in L.A. to Chicago to protest in that big march?"

"Yep." Joshua nodded as he began to devour another hot wing. "My wife and I were worried sick that whole day. We didn't hear anything from him until late that evening when he finally called and said that he was alright. He'd just been released from the hospital for minor injuries, but he said that some members in his group had been shot up pretty bad and were taken to the hospital and were still in critical condition. One of his friends from his group even got killed. That was just terrible to hear . . . so terrible."

"What do you think that this Purification Of America Today is trying to prove by bombing those Muslim mosques and those abortion clinics, and killing up protesters at the Black Unity Coalition march and those atheists marching in Washington D. C.? What do you think they're trying to say?"

"I think they're saying they're at war with this country. They're trying to rid America, in their opinion, of all the so called undesirables. And they mean business."

The phone in the office began to ring. Big Sam looked around; his restaurant staff wasn't anywhere nearby.

"Let me get this phone."

While Joshua was left alone, he began to tear into his hot wings like a man who'd been on a week-long hunger strike. Not only did Big Sam make the best ribs, but his hot wings would leave a hungry man begging for more.

When Joshua began to wipe his fingers with a napkin, Big Sam suddenly came back to the bar with a cordless phone in his hand.

"Somebody is on the phone for you," Big Sam said with a skeptical laugh. "The person said his name is Ben Franklin."

Joshua literally froze as he stared at Big Sam. He slowly took the phone as Big Sam came out from behind the bar and headed into the dining area as he began to socialize with a few other customers eating.

For the longest, Joshua just held the phone in his hand, too petrified to answer it as he remembered the strange call that he'd received late Saturday night. He'd pretty much put the call out of his mind by Sunday morning and had viewed it as nothing but a prank call, but now as he held the phone, something inside of him suddenly began to fear the worst.

"Yes . . . hello?" he finally answered.

"Enjoying the ribs?"

"Who is this?"

"Ben Franklin."

Joshua immediately recognized the voice. It was the same old raspy voice from the guy who'd called him midnight Saturday.

"And just who the hell is Ben Franklin?"

"The leader of our great patriotic organization, Purification Of America Today."

Joshua slowly looked around the establishment. The few restaurant patrons eating weren't paying him any attention as he sat alone at the bar. Big Sam had even disappeared. He was nowhere to be found.

"Why are you calling me?"

"Because, Mr. Joshua Edwards, I'm about to make you a superstar."

"What are you talking about?"

"Come tomorrow, you're going to be the biggest name in the news industry."

"I don't understand."

"Well, I'll explain it to you," the voice said in a gruff voice. "Come tomorrow, Purification Of America Today will continue its quest of purging America clean."

"I don't follow you."

"You know the American female swimmer who just won the gold medal in the Olympics who had an abortion earlier this year so she wouldn't miss the chance to swim in the Olympic Games?"

"Yes."

"Good. Now, are you familiar with that TV comedy show Ellington Place that comes on every Wednesday night with those two goofball actors who portray being gay and married to one another?"

"Somewhat."

"Good, because tomorrow we're going to kill all three of them. And not only that, we're going to kill a famous network news anchorman who supports the LGBT community, a federal judge who recently blocked school prayer from being allowed in several states, and we're also going to bomb a welfare office."

Joshua held the phone in his hand and couldn't believe what he'd just heard. He once again glanced around the rib joint; no one was paying him any attention.

"Who is this?" Joshua said more firmly into the phone.

"Come now, Mr. Edwards." The caller began to chuckle. "Must we still play these useless, silly games?"

"Why are you doing this?"

"Because America must be cleansed of all of the corrupt, dirty filth that has taken over this once great land. Our values have been encroached upon by a deviant culture that must be eradicated. The world is watching us, and we must become that beacon of light that we once were. We were once America the beautiful and America the great. We were the home of the innocent and the home of apple pie, and we must get that back."

"Why are you telling me all of this?" Joshua said in a confused voice. "What's the purpose of this phone call?"

"I've read your blog many times. And though I don't agree with your views, you're very good, Mr. Edwards."

"And what's that supposed to mean?"

"It means I believe in affirmative action, at least just this once," the caller said with a chuckle.

"And what does that mean?"

"It means I'm going to give you the chance to be the biggest name in the news business," the caller said without fluff. "I'm giving you the chance to write in your blog everything that I just told you today so that all your followers will get the news straight from you first. And come tomorrow, when it all comes to fruition, you'll be the biggest soothsayer or fortune teller this world has ever seen."

Joshua held the phone for the longest in complete utter shock. "You're crazy," he finally answered in a nervous voice. "I can't write something like that in my blog. You're insane!"

"I'm not insane, Mr. Edwards," the caller said in a cool voice. "I'm just telling you what's going to be."

"Are you some kind of lunatic calling me up spouting off some wild, ludicrous stories or something?" Joshua suddenly said in a heated voice. "Besides, how do I *really* know that you're some member of some Purification Of America Today? How do I know that this isn't some crazy prank call?"

"I guess you'll find that out tomorrow, won't you, Mr. Edwards?"

The caller suddenly hung up. Long after the conversation had ended, Joshua still held the phone staring at it in speechless silence.

Chapter 4

The next morning Joshua was rudely awakened out of a beautiful, blissful dream. He slowly opened his eyes and saw his wife standing over him as she pounded the living daylights out of his chest while he lay in bed. It took a couple of seconds for Joshua to focus his still sleepy eyes on his wife.

As his eyes slowly focused, his wife began to look like a panicked pedestrian on the side of the road who'd just witnessed the worst car wreck of her life. She pointed wildly and erratically while her mouth moved a hundred miles an hour, but her words were totally muted.

"What is it, Faye?" Joshua finally said as consciousness slowly began to take over.

"Look at what's happening!" his wife's panicked voice finally had volume as she desperately pointed toward the TV. "It's unbelievable!"

Joshua slowly sat up in his bed and focused on the TV in his bedroom. Breaking news suddenly reported that a welfare office in Cincinnati had just been bombed as ten people were reported killed; United States Federal Judge Sherman Limenski had just been assassinated; Mark Hanker and Joey Fillmore, the stars of the hit comedy show, Ellington Place, had been murdered; Olympic gold medal swimmer Debby Smith was found dead in her car from a gunshot wound to her head; and long time news anchorman Bill Killerman's home had been bombed this morning and he was found dead inside.

With his heart beginning to race, Joshua yanked the television remote from his wife's hand and began to flip through all the channels. Every cable news network was reporting the tragedy that had just unfolded. Word quickly spewed over the TV that it was once again the extremist organization, Purification Of America Today, claiming responsibility for the attacks.

Joshua quickly rose out of bed as he went and stood directly in front of the TV in his pajamas. He stared at the screen in disbelief. The unbelievable moment he watched seemed to suddenly put his body in freeze lock as the TV remote slowly slipped from his hand and fell to the floor.

"What in the world is going on in this country?" Faye said as she stood beside Joshua. They both stared at the TV screen as the ongoing breaking news continued. "This is just awful."

"Oh, my God," Joshua said as his voice became hoarse with fear. "That phone call really was from Purification Of America Today. Oh, my God!"

Joshua rushed to the nightstand by the bed, grabbed his cellphone, and quickly dialed the number to the police.

Two hours later, Joshua's parlor became filled with police officers and several agents from the Federal Bureau of Investigation. They grilled him with all kinds of questions concerning the mysterious caller who'd contacted him. Joshua sat on his couch staring at all of these police officers and agents from the FBI as he tried to answer their questions the best he could.

"Now, Mr. Edwards, you said this caller first called you Saturday night around midnight after the initial attacks had occurred Saturday afternoon?" one of the FBI agents asked as he took notes.

"Yes, that's right. He called himself George Washington and said he was from the Purification Of America Today organization."

"What did he say?"

"He said that for the next several weeks we were going to become pretty close."

"Did he give a reason?"

"He said something to the effect that he had read my blog, Justice For All, numerous times and said that I was one of the reasons why America must go through a cleansing and purification because of quote 'liberals like me'. That's what he said."

"Why do you believe that he contacted you specifically?"

"I don't have any idea," he said as he looked around at all the agents and police officers in his parlor. "But if I were to guess, I'd say because I'm a black journalist, and he sees that I'm the other voice or the other side to his cause. And I think it's something of a game that he's playing."

"What did he sound like?"

"He had an old raspy voice. He talked with a lot of confidence and even kind of laughed and chuckled after saying a couple of things. It was kind of strange."

"Now when he called you yesterday, where were you?" another agent asked.

"I was at the rib joint that I often frequent in the Crenshaw area called Sam's Rib Shack."

"He called you on your cellphone?"

"No, he called the phone at Sam's Rib Shack. Sam Shell, who runs the place and who everybody loves to call Big Sam, answered the phone and said someone named Ben Franklin wanted to speak with me."

"Ben Franklin?" the agent said. "Not George Washington?"

"No, this time it was Ben Franklin."

"Have you noticed anyone following you lately?"

"Not that I can tell."

"What did this phone call entail?"

"The guy said that he was going give me the chance to become, in his words, a superstar. He wanted me to write in my blog yesterday what was going to happen today concerning the murders that he said that Purification Of America Today was going to commit. And by doing so, I would be viewed as some kind of great fortune teller of the predicted tragedy to come."

"So he specifically told you of the people who were going to be murdered?"

"He mentioned the Olympic swimmer who'd had an abortion earlier this year so she wouldn't miss the Olympic Games. He mentioned the two actors from the show Ellington Place who portrayed being gay and married on the show to one another. He also mentioned they were going to kill a federal judge, a news anchorman, and bomb a welfare office."

"Did he say why?"

"He said that America must be cleansed of all of the corrupt, dirty filth that has taken over this great land. He started spouting off that our values have been encroached upon by a deviant culture that must be eradicated."

"Mr. Edwards, why didn't you contact the authorities yesterday after talking to this person?"

"I really didn't know what to make of the conversation we had," Joshua said defensively. "I truly thought it was some prank caller spouting off at the mouth, playing some kind of trick. Then I saw what happened this morning and realized the severity of the situation. You got to believe me, it truly hurt seeing what happened to those people and realizing that I had just talked to the person who told me exactly what was going to happen."

"Did the caller say when or if he would try to contact you again?"

"No, he didn't."

"Mr. Edwards, what specific topics do you write about in your blog?"

"I talk about social problems, race issues, problems with the criminal justice system, equality issues, class struggles, police brutality, politics, religious matters, and a number of many other things."

"Anything that can be considered subversive?"

"Subversive?" Joshua said with a frown. "Absolutely not."

"Anything that would incite any hard core rebellious tendencies in extremist hate groups to try to counter or try to act out against?"

"Definitely not."

"Mr. Edwards—"

Faye suddenly opened the parlor door. She stuck her head in, interrupting the private meeting as she looked at Joshua sitting on the couch.

"Joshua," Faye said with a trace of hesitation, "you got an important call on the house line."

"I can't come to the phone now, Faye," Joshua said with frustration as he quickly waved his hand at all the police officers and FBI agents crammed in his parlor. "You're going to have to take a message."

"The caller told me to tell you that it was Thomas Jefferson," she said with a trace of fear in her voice, "and he said it was mighty important."

Joshua's eyes immediately grew wide. Without hesitating, he quickly rose from the couch as he went to the phone on a stand near the fireplace. He glanced at the police officers and FBI agents for a second, then slowly turned to the phone. He put the call on speakerphone so the officers and agents in the room could hear. At the moment, the room was so still and quiet, Joshua could literally hear his heart beating.

"Joshua Edwards here," he said in a loud voice toward the speakerphone.

"Mr. Edwards, Thomas Jefferson here," the caller said. Joshua immediately recognized the old, raspy voice. "Have you seen the news today?"

"Yes, I have."

"I told you if you would've written what I told you yesterday, you'd be the biggest celebrity in the country at this very moment. Now do you believe that I'm from Purification Of America Today?"

"Yes."

"I thought you would," the voice said in an arrogant tone. "Now, I got something else I want to tell you."

Joshua slowly glanced at the police officers and FBI agents in the parlor. They all listened intently. "And what is that?"

"Purification Of America Today isn't finished with purifying this great country, not by a long shot. We're about to execute the next phase of our great plan. We're about to bomb a couple of public schools in cities all across this country. And I'm sad to say that a lot of kids are going to die."

"Why are you doing this?"

"Because we must. The corruption of our schools by so many of these transgender kids perverting the minds of the good, decent kids, the teaching of evolution, the promiscuity of sex in school with children now having babies, and so many other corrupt, debase values that our school system has chosen to promote or ignore altogether must be dealt with. And it must be dealt with now before it's too late."

"But you'll be killing innocent children who haven't done anyone any harm."

"We're in a war, Mr. Edwards," the voice said in an ominous tone. "Yes, there'll be some innocent children who'll die, but in war, both the innocent and the evil go down by the sword. But the goal will be achieved."

"Why are you telling me all of this?" Joshua said as his voice suddenly became strained. "Why have you sought me out to lay this on me?"

"I told you, Mr. Edwards, affirmative action," the caller said with a slight chuckle. "Just this once, I believe in it."

The caller suddenly hung up. Joshua turned off the speakerphone and slowly gazed around the parlor at everyone. All the FBI agents in the room had snatched out their cellphones as they made urgent calls.

Chapter 5

News about the impending threat to bomb public schools in cities across the nation immediately began to spread through the news cycles. Not only did the major news networks begin to issue alerts and warnings, but social media quickly exploded into a mad frenzy. With what had already taken place over the last few days, the nation desperately wanted to ward off another devastating attack. Even more, it desperately wanted to try to save the lives of the nation's youth from being harmed.

The threat was taken so seriously that the President of the United States immediately issued an order to close all public schools across the nation for the remainder of the week. Not since 9/11 when all air traffic across the nation was grounded and halted had such an order virtually shut down a vital institution in America. Within hours, the threat had become the nation's prime number one issue, and the extremist hate group, Purification Of America Today, had become the nation's number one enemy.

Joshua quickly became front and center stage across America. Within hours of the story bursting onto the American public, everyone from Maine to California wanted to know why Purification Of America Today had contacted him. Newspapers and radio stations across the country began to besiege him with endless phone calls. He had dozens of requests to come on talk shows to be interviewed and questioned about the situation. Like lightning in a bottle, he was suddenly in hot demand. Even the followers to his weekly blog rose dramatically. In just twenty-four hours, he'd gone from two million faithful followers to over ten million!

However, Joshua quickly resisted going before the cameras to do any interviews. He didn't want to create any hysteria over this tragic situation or fuel the fire for any sensational stories to spring forth off the backs of young children across the country who could be in grave danger. More than anything, he didn't want to become what Purification Of America Today desperately wanted him to become; some vain superstar in their corrupt, warped eyes. He wasn't about to play their dirty little game, because he knew more than anyone that their game was treacherous and deadly.

Joshua, for the sake of America's children, decided to stay low. He wasn't going to do any TV interviews, no radio requests, no roundtable talks, or no town hall discussions. Joshua wasn't even going to blog. He decided to let tensions around the country die down before he spoke on the issue at hand.

Chapter 6

Sunday afternoon, Joshua and Faye arrived home from church as Faye began to prepare for Sunday dinner. Joshua almost thought he was going to have to hold a press conference today after church. Soon as church service ended, everyone immediately began hounding him about the situation concerning Purification Of America Today.

Everyone wanted to know every little detail and snippet said to him when he was contacted. It was like the media had suddenly showed up at church starving for some answers, but Joshua was not about to divulge anything to his church brothers and sisters that wasn't circulating in the media already. His fellow church brethren would just have to be upset with him, like everyone else across the nation was upset with him, for not divulging what they wanted to hear.

While Faye busied herself over the stove in the kitchen preparing Sunday dinner, Joshua entered the kitchen and opened the refrigerator. He grabbed a pitcher of iced tea that Faye had just made, poured himself a glass, and had a seat at the kitchen table.

"When I was changing clothes upstairs in the bedroom, I had the news on," Joshua said as he looked at his wife while she cooked at the stove. "The President said all public schools will be opening back up tomorrow."

"Well, it's been six days now since you got that phone call," Faye said as she continued cooking. "Everything has been pretty calm around the country. No schools have been bombed or anything. Schools can't stay closed forever."

"Yeah, I just hope and pray nothing will happen."

"I'm sure all the schools will have protection."

"They said they're going to protect all schools as best as they can. All public schools around the country will have massive police protection. The sheriff's departments around the country will be out in force, state troopers will be patrolling, all governors in their states will be sending out their National Guard to safeguard the children tomorrow, and even the President is ordering various divisions of the army to patrol areas near schools around the country. It's going to be like the Little Rock Nine back in 1957, only on a massive, larger scale."

"Sounds like the schools are going to be well protected tomorrow."

"Yeah, but we're talking about thousands and thousands of public schools around the nation. All the armies in the world can't cover every single public school in this country," Joshua said in a pessimistic voice. He drained his glass of iced tea and rose from the kitchen table. "I'm going to head upstairs and watch the news for a while. How long before dinner?"

"About an hour."

"Kahila and Tyesha coming over?"

"Yeah, they'll be coming as usual," Faye said as she slowly turned from the stove and glanced at Joshua with concern while he headed out of the kitchen. "And I also invited your brother, Conrad, and his wife, Lacy, over to eat, too."

Joshua stopped in the kitchen doorway. He quickly spun around and glared at Faye. "You did what?"

"Now, Joshua, please don't get upset," Faye said in an easy voice. "I haven't invited them over for dinner in nearly a year. And you and your brother need to start learning how to get along with each other."

"What the hell did you do that for?" he said with a frown. "You know every time he comes over it just ends up one big old mess."

"Not today it won't," Faye said as she eyed him, "because you're going to promise me that you're going to see to it that nothing gets started. Correct?"

"Faye—"

"Is that a promise?"

"Faye, I can't believe you—"

"Is that a promise?" she said while slowly folding her arms and continuing to give him a stern, unwavering look.

Joshua finally threw up his hands in frustration as he turned and stormed out of the kitchen. He quickly climbed the winding staircase and bolted upstairs. When he entered his bedroom, he flopped onto his bed and turned on the TV to the news as he kept the sound on mute.

More than anything, Joshua dreaded having dinner with his family on Sundays. Though he loved his two children dearly, his relationship with his kids was shaky at best. There was somewhat of a strained distance that he had with his two children that had only become more strained as time had gone by.

The trouble that Joshua had with each of his two children was quite complex. His son, Kahila, at age twenty-three, grew up a wild, rebellious kid. Lecturing, punishments, even downright beatings did absolutely nothing to quell his rebellious, wild ways.

When Joshua began to attain the means of the affluent life when his blog started becoming successful, he finally sent Kahila away for a couple of years of his adolescent life to boarding school to try to tame his uncontrollable nature. Sending Kahila away to boarding school, however, did nothing to quell his rebellious tendencies. It only made him more rebellious, and on top of that, it made Kahila have a burning hatred and a disdain for Joshua for sending him away that he still carried around with him to this very day.

Kahila's wild rebellious ways eventually led to him dropping out of school at age sixteen and getting into trouble with the law. By eighteen, he was in and out of jail for selling drugs and for even theft. At twenty, he got caught up in a bad dope deal and ended up killing the intended person who tried to rob him. Joshua hired Kahila a good lawyer who was able to get his son off from the potential murder conviction, but Kahila's unruly ways never changed.

Joshua continued to try to mentor to his wayward son and find him meaningful employment, but nothing ever worked. The only thing that seemed to begin to stabilize Kahila was when he joined the Black Unity Coalition organization.

Through his involvement with the Black Unity Coalition, Kahila slowly began to find his purpose and mission in life. The drugs and his wild rebellious way of life began to fade away somewhat when he took up the noble mantle of fighting injustice and inequality that inflicted the black race. He began to find his calling in life, but his relationship with his father remained strained.

On the other hand, Tyesha, at age twenty-one, did well in school growing up. She followed her father's footsteps, majored in journalism in college, and had recently graduated with a journalism degree; however, her sexuality became a sticky issue with Joshua and Faye.

The attraction that Tyesha had for the same sex quickly became apparent to Faye and Joshua at an early age in their daughter's life, and it was one they couldn't accept. Joshua tried many times during his daughter's teenage years to introduce her to male friends to try to dissuade her from liking the same sex, but it only made Tyesha abhor her father's infringement upon her life.

Tyesha rebelled against Joshua's meddlesome ways by dating and becoming involved with as many female lovers that she came across, which only made the relationship with Joshua more strained as he continued to push for a change in his daughter's life. Within time, she became even more resolute in her stand to live her life the way she wanted.

To further her commitment, Tyesha soon began to take up the cause of others like her going through similar situations. She, and a couple of other kindred souls determined to give a voice to their point of view, started an Internet blog called New Day, which motivated and gave support to young lesbian women looking for inspiration in the modern twenty-first century. Joshua, tired of the discontent and not wanting to cause a further rift in the relationship that he had with Tyesha, eventually raised the white flag and called a truce.

Now, in a little under an hour, they were all getting ready to sit down together as a family and have Sunday dinner. Joshua knew, whenever the family got together, there was bound to be some friction and discord around the dinner table. On top of that, with his difficult, irritable brother, Conrad, and his wife coming over to dine with the family today, there was definitely a good chance for some sparks to fly.

An hour later, the Edward extended family all sat together in the dining room having Sunday dinner. Joshua sat at the head of the dining table while Faye sat at the opposite end. Kahila and Tyesha sat on one side of the dining table as Conrad and his wife, Lacy, sat on the other side.

Joshua truly dreaded whenever his brother came to his house for dinner, knowing the potential friction that it could cause. To smooth over his deep anxiety for his brother's company, he even decided to break his ten year ban against alcohol. He elected to have a little red wine with his meal today to somewhat intoxicate away the presence of his older brother, but the need for any spirits didn't seem necessary. The setting at the dining table was pretty much amicable as the six of them ate and tried to make pleasant conversation. There didn't seem to be any animosity whatsoever.

"So, Lacy, how are things with Los Angeles' social welfare system these days?" Joshua asked. He'd just finished his steak as he sipped from his glass of red wine. "You've been with our city's social welfare department for twenty years, haven't you?"

"Twenty-three to be exact," Lacy said as she finished her meal. "And I've just been promoted to head executive supervisor of our children's welfare department."

"Congratulations," Faye said with a smile as she raised her glass of red wine in a gesture of a toast. "I know from working with you for a number of years that you've worked hard for a long time. The City of L.A. deserves good leadership in our social services."

"Amen." Joshua added with a smile while he also raised his glass of wine.

"Thanks," Lacy said with a huge smile. "I only hope I can serve as a good administrator for this city, because a good children's social service is a dire must for a big city with all the problems that we have on a constant basis. We've got misplaced abandoned children on the rise every day, and the number of runaways is also escalating. The state of our foster care system needs a major overhaul, and there are so many other grave issues that we need to address. There's just so much that needs to improve."

"I know," Faye said as she looked at Lacy. "We see it every day at A Hand In Need. Our organization has been trying to raise donations for months for our national homeless campaign. We know so many children are affected with homeless issues across this nation every day. It's a must that we try to help every child in need to get the basics of food, clothing, and shelter."

"I saw you on the news last week talking about your organization's national conference that's coming up," Lacy said with interest. "When is it supposed to be?"

"It's at the end of next month in New York. We're going to be there for four days at our annual convention. And so far our twenty regional chapters across the country have raised over three million dollars for the homeless this year."

"That's wonderful."

The conversation suddenly began to wane as everyone began to sit back and sip from their wine glasses. Everyone had virtually finished their steaks, baked potato, and asparagus. The wine was the only thing, for the moment, consumed around the dining table. Kahila and Tyesha, who weren't very talkative, seemed bored by the whole dinner affair as they refilled their wine glasses and kept silent. Conrad had finished his meal twenty minutes ago and was already on his fourth refill of wine.

"Well," Faye said as she looked at everyone with a smile. "I think it's time we had our dessert. Is anyone ready for some chocolate alamode? We can—"

"The hell with this," Conrad suddenly said with a huff as he threw his napkin down onto his empty plate. He leaned back in his chair as his huge belly protruded over his belt.

"We've all been sitting around here talking about a bunch of nonsense," Conrad said as he slowly looked around at everyone. He then fixed his stare directly on Joshua at the head of the table. "But what I want to know is what the hell did this guy from Purification Of America Today say to you when he called, and why the hell did he call you of all people?"

"Conrad," his wife suddenly said as she turned and glared at him. "Now we didn't come here to discuss none of that."

"The hell we didn't," Conrad said with a snap.

"Conrad—"

"Damnit, be quiet, Lacy!" he said with a sneer. He turned his gaze back to Joshua, who sat at the head of the table in total silence. "Well?"

Joshua slowly drank from his glass of wine for the longest as he ignored his brother. "Why don't you have another glass of wine, Conrad," he finally said. "In fact, Faye, get out another bottle of wine for Mr. Edwards over here. Maybe he'll get so drunk he'll fall face-first into his plate."

"I thought *you* didn't drink at all anymore."

"Only an occasional glass of wine every blue moon when I'm in the company of good folk," Joshua said with a bit of sarcasm as he looked at his brother.

"Maybe we should go, Conrad," Lacy said with a pained expression. "We've had a lovely time, and there's no need of spoiling it with you and Joshua arguing with one another."

"No, Lacy." Conrad snapped angrily as he looked at his wife. "They invited us over, so let's have a discussion."

"I agree," Kahila suddenly said as he peered straight at Joshua. "We're all family here. What the hell you got to hide from us?"

Joshua gave Kahila a stern look, but Kahila kept his unwavering gaze straight on his father.

"Look, he said pretty much what the country already knows," Joshua finally said in a reluctant voice while everyone listened. "He said that they were going to bomb schools in cities across the nation because of how corrupt our public schools had become over the years. He named a bunch of other stuff such as transgender kids perverting the minds of all the other decent kids, the teaching of evolution in schools, all the promiscuity in schools with kids having kids, and just a general corrupt, debased system he says that our public school system has become. He was just ranting on and on like the pure nut that he and his fellow co-conspirators are."

"But why did this man just up and arbitrarily call you of all people in the world to tell you this information?" Conrad said in a hostile voice. "It makes no sense."

"Because he said he's read my wonderful, thought-provoking blog," Joshua said with a smug look as he stared at his brother.

"Because he's read your blog?"

"That and affirmative action."

"What?"

Joshua grabbed the wine bottle from the table and refilled his glass as he took a long, slow sip of wine that seemed to irritate his brother. It had been a long time since he'd had any alcohol, but today it seemed well worth it. Joshua thoroughly enjoyed irking Conrad. It gave him sort of a weird-like pleasure.

"What the hell you talking about, Josh?" Conrad finally said in a steamed voice.

Joshua set his wine glass down and stared at his brother. "Look, the guy is sick and perverted. I don't know why he called me and laid this heavy burden on my chest. The guy has a twisted mind and he's playing games. He claims the reason why these attacks are happening is because of liberals like me who have somehow brought the country down because of our views. He calls himself all of these Founding Father names when he calls for some crazy reason. The guy is nothing but a sick, twisted freak."

"The guy may be a sick, twisted freak, but he's certainly right," Conrad said as he glared at Joshua and pointed his finger at him. "All you damn wayward liberals have done nothing but set this country on a path of decadent destruction. You and all your cronies like you, with the power of your pen and your words, have virtually destroyed the integrity of this country."

"What?"

"That's right," Conrad said with fire in his eyes. "Just look at the moral fiber of this country over the last decade and how debased and immoral it's become. Liberals like you have put this country in the state that it's in."

"You're actually going to sit there and agree with that mad, evil organization that calls themselves Purification Of America Today? You're going to sit there and believe they're right by going around bombing and killing up innocent people because our views are not their views?"

"Absolutely not," Conrad said as he quickly shook his head. "But just look at what has taken place over the last several years because the liberal movement has pushed its way across this country. We have constant social and racial unrest, rights of the people are slowly being taken away, we have these abortion advocates literally banging down the doors of people's homes pushing their agenda down the throats of everyone, we have this marriage equality running rampant throughout the country—"

"Now wait a minute," Tyesha said as she suddenly eyed Conrad across the table. "The law of this country states that same sex marriages are the constitutional right of any couple who chooses to unite together no matter what gender they may be. Besides, a majority of Americans in this country now support the legal recognition of same sex marriages. So that argument that marriage equality is not the opinion of the people rings hollow and doesn't represent the views of the majority of the people in this country."

"Which is exactly what I'm talking about how the liberal movement has persuaded a large populace of people in this country that marriage equality is acceptable," Conrad argued. "This movement has—"

"Excuse me!" Tyesha said pointedly as she suddenly held up her finger. "But the law says that if I want to marry the person of my choice, if it be the same sex or not, then I'm perfectly in my right to do so."

"Tyesha, let's just drop this subject," Joshua said as he glared at his hostile daughter. "Now is not the time for this discussion."

"Discuss what?" Tyesha said as she turned and looked at Joshua. "About me marrying Patricia?"

"Yes."

"Well, I say let's discuss it right now."

"No, we're not."

"Why? You're afraid that me and Patricia will be getting married if we happen to discuss it?"

"Tyesha, now is not the time for this."

"You know, I think Patricia and I have been engaged long enough. I think it's high time that we finally got married," Tyesha said in a cocksure voice as she poured herself another glass of wine. "Now is as good a time as any. What do you think, daddy dearest?"

"Tyesha—"

"You know, I think we'll have us a nice, big wedding."

"Tyesha—"

"Yes, let's see," she said as she set her wine glass down and began to ponder. "I'll invite all of my friends and lots and lots of guests."

"Tyesha—"

"Maybe we'll get married next month. Yes, next month sounds perfect," she said to herself with a satisfied smile. "So, I guess I need to start getting my guest list ready and Patricia will need to get her list ready, too. We need to go ahead and book the hotel where we'll be having the wedding. Oh, and Daddy," she said as she looked at Joshua, "you'll need to go ahead and put a down payment for the hotel and a down payment for a good caterer, and—"

"Tyesha, I will not allow you to marry that girl!" Joshua suddenly exploded. "And that's final!"

Everyone at the table stared at Tyesha in total silence. The silence was like a heavy, thick fog so thick that it made communicating with one another virtually impossible.

Tyesha, during the awkward silence that hovered over the dining room, took a long, slow sip from her glass of wine and smacked her lips with content when she finally finished. She then looked at Joshua who had defiant, authoritative look as he glared at his daughter.

"Well, I'm afraid you're a little too late, daddy dearest," Tyesha said with a cunning smile, "because, you see, Patricia and I have already said our wedding vows."

"What?"

"That's right, daddy dearest," she said as her smile widened. "We took our vows together when we went to Las Vegas last week and now we're officially married."

"No, Tyesha," Faye suddenly said from the other end of the table as she gawked at her daughter in disbelief. "Please don't say it's so. It can't be true."

"Yes, Mother, it's most definitely a bona fide true fact," she said as she pulled out the marriage license from her pocket and proudly waved it around so everyone at the table could see.

Joshua glared at Tyesha for the longest, then rose slowly from the table as he started to head out of the dining room.

"See what I mean?" Conrad began to rant at Joshua as he was leaving the dining room. "That's what this new free willing liberalism movement has done to this young generation of this country. It's perverted their minds and affected your own daughter. Do you hear me?" he yelled as Joshua began to climb the winding staircase as he headed upstairs. "You better listen to me!"

Once Joshua entered his bedroom, he closed the door and flopped onto his bed. He grabbed the remote from the nightstand and turned on his widescreen TV. Quickly realizing he wasn't in the mood to hear anything, he clicked the remote and turned off the set.

He realized that he needed total, utter silence to deal with the shock that had just been thrown into his face.

Chapter 7

Monday morning Joshua arrived at nine o'clock sharp for his monthly appointment to see his psychiatrist, Dr. Harold L. Mitchell. For the past twelve years, Joshua had been going to see a psychiatrist after his battle with depression. Twelve years ago he went every week, then biweekly, then eventually down to only once a month.

A couple of years ago, Dr. Mitchell indicated that he didn't need to see Joshua anymore because he had fully recovered from the demons torturing him, but Joshua refused. He wanted to continue his visits with Dr. Mitchell. He'd gotten used to his monthly visits over the years to see his psychiatrist, and it made him feel good when he left from one of his visits. Plus, his psychiatrist had virtually become a good friend the last several years. He was like a good shoulder that Joshua liked to lean on from time to time.

Twelve years ago when Joshua first started seeing his psychiatrist, he was a mess. He'd just been released from his position as a political journalist for the *Washington Star*, the newspaper he worked for, and had returned to Los Angeles. He and Faye had just separated after an affair he'd had with another woman. She'd taken the kids and had moved across town. Joshua couldn't find another job as a journalist anywhere, and he was depressed and drinking heavily. For an entire year Faye wouldn't let him see the kids and she was divorcing him. Times were tough, and Joshua constantly drowned his problems away with his drinking.

Finally one night Joshua got really drunk and checked into a motel. He took a handful of tranquilizers and his gun with him with intentions of potentially doing himself bodily harm. When Joshua was found the next morning in his motel room on the floor with the gun lying on his chest and the empty bottle of tranquilizers beside him, he was rushed to the hospital.

After recovering in the hospital and spending a short stint in a mental institution, Joshua began to see a psychiatrist for depression. Faye decided not to go through with the divorce and chose to stick by Joshua through the brutal times. Taking it day by day and being persistent on going forward, Joshua slowly began to put his life back together as he worked through his problems. Within a year, he was well on the road to full recovery.

Joshua began to get back on his feet as he commenced searching for meaningful employment. He banned himself from drinking and refocused his career objective. Wanting to get back at what he knew best, which was journalism, Joshua started his blog, Justice For All, and it slowly began to grow. With hard work and diligence, he'd reclaimed his life and was doing what he loved to do. Now twelve years later, he was virtually on top of the world as millions around the country waited each week to hear what he had to say.

After checking in with the secretary for his appointment for the day, Joshua was escorted into Dr. Harold L. Mitchell's office. Dr. Mitchell was a tall, distinguishing looking man at sixty-five. He met Joshua at his office door with a cheerful smile as they shook hands like old friends. Joshua was accustomed to the good camaraderie that he and his psychiatrist had together over the years. They were like good brothers who mutually respected one another and cared for each other's well-being.

"Joshua, you're looking well today," Dr. Mitchell said with a hearty smile as he greeted Joshua at the door. "How's the past thirty days been treating you?"

"Quite well," Joshua said as he smiled back at Dr. Mitchell. "A few strange oddities have recently popped into my life these last few days. But I guess all is well."

"Yes, I've heard you've been quite the popular person lately. Some nasty eccentric people who want to do our country harm have been whispering into your ear."

"That's putting it mildly," Joshua said with a smirk. "Seems like over the last several days, I've been having conversations with the dark angel himself who wants to tell me all of his wicked, evil secrets."

"That certainly must be an unpleasant burden," Dr. Mitchell said with a bemused smile. "Anything else interesting that's happened?"

"Yeah, I broke my ten year ban and had a little red wine with my Sunday meal yesterday."

"Oh, really?" Dr. Mitchell chuckled. "Well, that's not so bad."

"In fact it was quite pleasant," Joshua said with a smile.

"I'm sure it was." Dr. Mitchell laughed. "Let's have a seat so we can talk a little further."

Joshua had a seat in a plush comfortable chair in front of Dr. Mitchell's beautifully crafted glass top desk while Dr. Mitchell went around his desk and had a seat.

Dr. Mitchell's office was almost a palace in of itself. The walls were decorated with all sorts of expensive fine art work that represented French culture at its best. An eight-foot sculpture of the Eifel Tower that looked as if it were made of pure gold stood in a corner and gave the office a resplendent feel to it. The view of downtown Los Angeles out the large office window was definitely a sight to behold. Dr. Mitchell's office exuded the feeling of walking through exquisite culture while sipping on the best champagne, but whatever feeling the office exuded, Dr. Mitchell's clients certainly paid a steep price for it.

"Well, Joshua, I know you've currently got quite an extraordinary situation on your hands that you're currently dealing with concerning this extremist group, Purification Of America Today, contacting you as they've been doing here lately," Dr. Mitchell said as he leaned back in his huge opulent chair and looked at Joshua with concern. "I'm sure you have a few things you'd like to get off your chest concerning that."

"That's been quite an extraordinary situation as you say, Dr. Mitchell," Joshua said slowly as he folded his arms. "But what I really wanted to talk to you about was my daughter."

"Your daughter," Dr. Mitchell said with a smile. "And how is Tyesha?"

"Well, she's doing well," Joshua said with reluctance in his voice. "But she just dropped something on me during our weekly Sunday family dinner at my house yesterday that kept my wife and me up all last night, tossing and turning in a literal nightmare."

"Oh . . . what would that be?"

"She told us that she got legally married to her girlfriend, Patricia, when she went to Las Vegas last week."

"I see," Dr. Mitchell said with a ponderous look. "And how did that make you feel?"

"It made me angry," Joshua said in a pained voice. "I've always known that Tyesha had lesbian friends, but I never thought she would one day become united in a legal marriage with one of her lesbian lovers. Quite frankly, I don't know if I can accept it."

"Is Tyesha still living with you and your wife?"

"No!" Joshua quickly shook his head. "Tyesha and Kayhila both have apartments and living their own lives. And quite frankly, if Tyesha were still living with me and my wife, I definitely wouldn't allow that sort of marriage to exist under my roof."

"You wouldn't?"

"Absolutely not," Joshua said firmly. "However, Tyesha is twenty-one and has her own place now. She has a right to do as she pleases, but I don't know if I can stand to have her married partner around during our weekly family Sunday dinners. I just don't know if I could look across my dinner table and accept that fact. But I don't want to create any distance between me and my daughter. I love Tyesha and I want us to stay a close family. There has to be a solution to this problem, Dr. Mitchell."

"The question you'll have to answer is how deeply do you love your daughter?"

"As deep as the ocean."

"How far would you go to save your daughter if she were in trouble?"

"To the far depths if I had to."

"If your daughter were hanging off the ledge of a steep cliff, would you pull her up to safety?"

"Of course I would."

"What if she were hanging off the ledge of a steep cliff and there was someone below her who was handcuffed to her wrist. Would you still try to pull her up to safety?"

"Yes."

"Even if you knew that the sheer weight of pulling both of them up from that ledge of that steep cliff would take a tremendous amount of strength and effort. Far more effort than it would take to pull just one person up. Would you still do it?"

"Yes, I still would."

"Then that's what you're going to have to do if you want to save and keep your daughter," Dr. Mitchell said as he eyed Joshua carefully. "You're going to have to pull both your daughter and the person she's handcuffed to up from the ledge of that steep cliff. And even though it will take a supreme amount of effort on your part to pull both of them up, if you don't, you'll lose your daughter for sure. You'll lose her because if that other person falls off that ledge of that steep cliff, your daughter will fall also, because she's handcuffed to the other person. Don't you see?"

Joshua stared at his psychiatrist for the longest in a dead silence. He slowly gazed up at the ceiling and let out a long, deep sigh. Finally he looked back at Dr. Mitchell.

"You always have a way of cutting straight to the chase," Joshua said in a somber voice. "Don't you, Doc?"

"That's what I'm here for," he said with a smile.

Joshua left Dr. Mitchell's office when his appointment was over as he hopped into his car and left out of downtown. As he drove along the busy L.A. freeway while he headed back home, he began to contemplate what Dr. Mitchell had said to him during his office visit. If he wanted to keep his daughter, he was going have to pull her up from the ledge of that steep high cliff, and since she was now handcuffed to someone else, he would have to pull both of them up if he wanted to save and keep his daughter.

The thought of looking at Tyesha and her new legal mate sitting together as newlyweds at his dining table during Sunday dinner, suddenly made Joshua's heart rumble and quake even harder than the Northridge earthquake. He didn't know if he saw them sitting together for the first time at his dining table, if he would take a blowtorch and literally try to pry those wretched handcuffs off that had them linked together and rule their marriage annulled.

Joshua, however, knew that solution, in the end, wouldn't work. Tyesha would only find a way to reunite those handcuffs back together and go on about her blissful way. Joshua knew he would just have to pull both of them up from that ledge and accept a new member within his family.

When Joshua finally entered his neighborhood and pulled into the driveway of his home, he immediately began to ponder the situation concerning the public schools. Today was the first day that public schools reopened around the country, and Joshua hoped and prayed that everything had gone alright. Surely with the heightened security blanketed around public schools all over the country this morning, everything had gone smoothly. Surely the kids around the country would be safe; at least Joshua dearly hoped they would be.

Joshua had barely opened the front door and had taken a few steps into the house when he immediately heard Faye's panicked call.

"Joshua, get up here!" Faye hollered from upstairs. "It's all over the news! Get up here!"

With his heart suddenly pounding like an earthquake and his blood rushing like a tsunami, Joshua bolted up the winding staircase. He quickly scurried into his bedroom breathing like a madman. Faye stood in front of their widescreen television as she stared at a breaking news report. The look on her face was stricken with pure horror.

"What's happened?" Joshua asked in a terrified voice as he stared at the TV. "Did they bomb a school? What happened?"

"No." Faye slowly shook her head as she continued to stare at the TV. "They didn't bomb a school."

"Well, what the hell happened?"

"They hit a daycare center in Detroit."

"They bombed a daycare center?"

"No," Faye slowly said as tears started rolling down her face. "They kidnapped seven little black children from an inner city daycare center in Detroit."

"Are you serious?" Joshua said in horror as he turned and gawked at Faye. "They kidnapped seven little black children from an inner city daycare center in Detroit?"

"Yes." Faye nodded as she wiped the stream of tears falling from her eyes. "Seven precious little black children taken at gunpoint."

"My goodness," Joshua exclaimed as he stared at the breaking news report on TV. "What in the world are those sick, twisted freaks going to do to those innocent children?"

While Joshua stood next to Faye as they both stared at the breaking news report on TV, Joshua's cellphone suddenly started ringing. Joshua reached into his pants pocket and pulled out his cellphone. He quickly looked at the caller ID on the cellphone and saw the word unavailable listed for the number. A dreaded fear instinctively came over him as he held the cellphone in his hand as it continued to ring. He slowly looked at Faye. Her lip began to quiver.

"Hello?" he nervously answered his cellphone.

"Hello, Mr. Edwards." It was the old raspy voice! "This is John Quincy Adams."

Joshua held the cellphone limply as he stared at Faye. He slowly nodded, confirming to Faye that it was the same caller. She suddenly slapped her hand over her mouth as she stared wide-eyed back at him. Joshua could feel his hand that gripped the cellphone beginning to become sweaty. It felt slimy and slippery.

"Why are you calling?"

"Well, I'm glad you're not asking who's calling anymore," the caller said with a wicked chuckle. "Have you seen the news?"

"Yes, I have."

"Then you know that's our work."

"Why are you doing this?"

"Well, we couldn't exactly execute our original plan with so much heightened security guarding the public schools, so we decided to execute another plan."

"You can't harm those kids."

"Well, that's all going to be up to you if they live or die."

"Me?" Joshua said in a frightened voice. "What are you talking about?"

"See, we executed this new plan with you in mind, Mr. Edwards," the caller said in a calm voice. "Seeing that these seven little kids have your race in common, we knew you'd be more inclined to do what we say in order to save them."

"What are you talking about?"

"Okay, this is how it's going to work," the caller said once again in a calm voice. "You'll meet in person on several different occasions at certain places with a contact person whom we'll be sending from Purification Of America Today. You'll interview that person on different topics and issues that will be prearranged. Are you following along so far?"

Joshua remained silent.

"Alright, after each interview, you'll write a rebuttal on the topic of discussion that you interviewed the contact person about in your blog to all of your followers," the caller said as he continued. "After each blog that's written on the prearranged topic of discussion, we'll release one of the kidnapped children unharmed."

"Is this some kind of crazy game?"

"We don't play games, Mr. Edwards," the caller suddenly said in a cold, sinister voice. "If you think we play games, we'll just go ahead and kill all seven little bastards that we've got right now to prove to you that we don't play around."

"No," Joshua suddenly said with his heart literally beating in his throat. "Please, don't do that."

A long silent pause ensued as Joshua held his cellphone gripped in his hand. He began to wonder was the caller going to say anything else.

"Now, Mr. Edwards, if you try to contact the police or FBI, we'll kill all seven children," the caller suddenly said in a firm voice. "And if you don't go through with what we're telling you, we'll kill every last child. Now, do you understand our terms?"

"Yes," Joshua said slowly. "But what assurance do I have that you'll actually release those kids after I write these blogs?"

"You'll just have to wait and see," the caller once again said in a calm voice. "But I'll guarantee you, we'll kill every last one if you don't do as we say."

"What's the purpose of doing this?"

"Because we as Purification Of America Today know why we're doing what we're doing," the caller said in a confident voice. "We have our reasons why America needs purifying. We're just giving the other side a chance to state their opinion on different issues concerning the state of America. That's why we're giving the other side a chance to rebut or refute our position."

"But why me?"

"Affirmative action, Mr. Edwards," he said with a slight chuckle. "You'll hear from us soon of where we'll meet and what the topic of our discussion will be. We'll be in contact."

The caller suddenly hung up. When the conversation ended, Joshua turned off his cellphone as he looked at his wife with a sickening feeling churning in his stomach.

Chapter 8

By eleven o'clock that night Joshua was alone in his study, and he was furious with Purification Of America Today for not only kidnapping and holding hostage innocent young black children, but for holding him *personally* responsible for their well-being and safety. These sick, twisted freaks had even emailed him within the last hour, pictures of the seven little children whom they had kidnapped and now currently held.

The faces of each of the seven children looked terrified, frightened, and lost as they were forced to pose for these unwanted photos. Some were even crying, no doubt begging their captors for the mercy of their mothers. Joshua had been staring at their pictures for the past hour, seething with a deep loathing like he'd never felt before. The loathing had now turned to pure hatred, and it burned in his heart. These sick twisted freaks, these ungodly monsters, were playing a dirty game with people's lives, and now it was time to strike back.

For the past week, Joshua had purposely not written an entry into his blog since the attacks first began. He didn't want to sensationalize the situation at hand, but his emotions had now boiled over and he couldn't hold back any longer. He had to say what was on his mind before the hatred boiling inside him, burned like wildfire, and totally scorched his soul.

Joshua sat at his computer eager to do what was on his mind. With the Internet already on, he logged onto his blog, went straight to a new entry page, and began to apply his fiery words to a new blog he'd entitled A Treacherous Evil That Needs Resolving. The words that he wanted to say to all of his followers literally burned through his fingers:

A Treacherous Evil That Needs Resolving

Over the past week, a treacherous evil has encroached upon our country. It has infringed upon our way of life, our culture, and our sense of freedom. This treacherous evil has manifested itself in a radical hate group that calls themselves Purification Of America Today.

These villainous scoundrels have taken upon themselves to play judge, jury, and executioner against the people of our great land that they deem as unfit or unworthy to live and express their way of life and their views as they see fit. This is not a totalitarian society where one group's views, culture, and way of life dominates the entire populace, that we all must align ourselves and march to the order of the drum of their voice. This is a free country with many voices and many views.

Nevertheless, these evil thugs, who call themselves Purification Of America Today, have declared war on all of us in this country who don't step in line with their views and who are of a different race, creed, and color. This is a crime against the integrity of every living soul in this country. The flag of the red, white, and blue stands for all to be free to express ourselves the way we feel as justice permits it, without fear of being condemned by any oppressor.

We, however, will fear no more. It is time to stand up and fight the oppressor. I call on all of those who feel persecuted and harassed by this evil, homegrown terrorist organization to sharpen your swords and hit the streets to protest against what this wretched evil organization stands for. The war that they started will be a war that we will end as victors.

Just like many before us who fought the oppressor from the Black Panthers fighting a corrupt police system, to the Jews fighting against the tyranny of the Holocaust, to women fighting for Women's suffrage, to runaway slaves fleeing for freedom in the Underground Railroad, we will stand and fight against this oppression. The war has commenced and it is time for battle. It is time for an eye for an eye and a tooth for a tooth!

When Joshua finished his blog and sent it off, his fingers felt like they were still on fire. There were even more words that he desperately wanted to say, but Joshua knew he'd said enough for one night. Tomorrow he'd find out the impact of what his words had as his followers logged onto his blog and read his new entry. He now had over ten million followers, virtually an entire army at his disposal, and his massive army was steadily growing by the day.

Chapter 9

With ten million followers to his blog, Joshua now had a huge megaphone and all of America was virtually listening. Within twenty-four hours of releasing his new blog, A Treacherous Evil That Needs Resolving, people from everywhere began to hit America's city streets to protest.

Huge, massive marches and demonstrations to protest what Purification Of America Today was doing began to spread across the country like a tsunami. Everywhere from Los Angeles, San Francisco, Seattle, Dallas, St. Louis, Chicago, Detroit, Atlanta, Washington, to New York, people demanded retribution. Everyone had heeded to the words sharpen your swords and hit the streets. The anger and sheer rage at what this sick, twisted organization was doing not only to the country, but to the defenseless children of America rumbled all over the country.

Angry protesters and demonstrators demanded that the government find this radical, racist organization and bring them to justice immediately, and if the government couldn't do the job, the people were ready for some vigilante justice. The war had indeed commenced, and in the eyes of angry protesters in cities across the country, it was time to stand up for what was right.

The loud call for justice from all the angry protesters and marchers, ironically, began to bring out sympathizers from other racist hate groups around the country who admired and supported what Purification Of America Today was doing. They also began to take to the streets of America to confront all the dissenters, protesters, and marchers who vehemently shouted through the streets for vengeance.

Radical racist hate groups with names like The Hell Saints, Salvation Renegades, Aryan Nation, White Power Front, Grand Allegiance To America, The Liberation Army, and even the Ku Klux Klan began to take to the streets of America to confront all the protesters and demonstrators. As tensions rose in the streets between these opposing entities, violent clashes and confrontations began to occur as fighting, gunfire, and other hostilities erupted in various places. Soon the violence led to all out rioting in many city streets as chaos exploded.

By the end of the week, after Joshua's fiery, divisive blog, America was literally burning. The streets of America had become a warzone of mayhem, bedlam, and pandemonium.

Joshua was in his bedroom Sunday night frantically packing for a flight he was preparing to take tomorrow morning for St. Louis. The caller from Purification Of America Today had called earlier and had given him specific instructions of where to meet the contact person they were sending for him to interview.

As he packed for tomorrow's trip, Joshua had the TV in the bedroom on the news. It showed coverage of all the violent clashes and rioting between protesters and all the various hate groups taking place in cities across the nation.

The house phone also constantly rang off the hook in his bedroom. Reporters from across the country called wanting to talk to him about his inflammatory blog that he'd just written that had caused all the chaos and mayhem in the streets across America, but Joshua didn't want to confront that at the moment. He felt terrible at what had transpired overnight in the streets of America and he now wished that he hadn't written such a divisive, incendiary blog; however, at the moment, he had more important things weighing on his mind.

Joshua was more than uneasy about flying to St. Louis tomorrow to meet with a member of Purification Of America Today. He didn't want to do some insane, senseless interview just to satisfy the whims of some evil twisted organization, but he just couldn't get the image of those seven kidnapped children out of his mind.

The images of those abducted children haunted Joshua every waking hour like an anchor around his neck. The pictures he'd been emailed several days ago of those children were constantly near him. He'd taken every last child to heart and now felt that it was his responsibility to get every last one of them freed. It was totally unfair to put that much of a burden on his shoulders, but there was no way around it. He simply had to go through the fire to save those precious little children.

"Joshua, this is totally insane," Faye suddenly said as she stood in the middle of their bedroom with her arms folded while she watched him pack. "What do you suppose to accomplish with this interview that you're going to be conducting?"

"I told you, Faye, they want me to interview them on different topics of discussion, and afterwards they want me to write a rebuttal piece on it in my blog. And after each blog that I write, they said they will release one of the kidnapped children unharmed."

"But that's simply ludicrous!"

"Faye, I know it's ludicrous," Joshua said angrily as he continued packing. "But we're not dealing with sane people. These people are a bunch of wacko nuts, but they have seven children—seven little *black* children—that they say they'll kill if I don't do as they say. I have no choice, Faye. I must go to St. Louis and do this interview."

"But you don't even know if these crazy nuts will actually release any of the children even if you do the interview and write about it in your blog," Faye said as she glared at him. "You're taking an incredible, dangerous risk by just hopping onto a plane and flying to St. Louis to meet with some contact person they're sending to meet with you. You could be walking into some kind of trap and be killed yourself."

"I realize that," Joshua said in a subdued voice. "But I know if I don't go, those children will be dead for sure."

"Well, where is this contact place that they want you to meet at when you get to St. Louis?"

"At this soul food diner called Kelsey's on the east side of St. Louis. I'm supposed to meet with the contact person at exactly noon tomorrow."

"A soul food diner?" Faye said as she gave Joshua an incredulous look. "A radical white supremacy hate group is sending someone to meet with you at a soul food diner for you to interview? You've got to be kidding?"

"Nope." Joshua shook his head. "I'm not kidding."

Faye let out a long sigh as she began to massage her temples. She glanced at the news on the TV and slowly shook her head.

"Look at what's going on in the streets, Joshua," Faye said in an exasperated voice. "This stuff is getting to be one huge mess. You're getting too involved in this, Joshua. You've got to pull back."

"Faye, I can't worry about all that stuff that's going on in the streets right now," he said as he closed his suitcase when he finished packing. "I know it's a terrible mess out there."

"Joshua, you can't meet with that person. You just can't do it!" Faye said as she suddenly approached him. "It's too dangerous!"

"Faye, I have to—"

The house phone began to ring for the twentieth time tonight. Joshua stormed over to the phone and answered it.

"Hello?"

"This is Stewart Anderson, editor of the *New York Pinnacle* magazine. I'd like to ask you a couple of questions concerning the recent article you wrote in your blog—"

"No comment."

Soon as Joshua hung up the phone, it started ringing again.

"Hello?" he answered with a rude tone.

"Yes, this is Phil Dershowitz of the *Boston Express*—"

"No comment!"

When Joshua hung up the phone, Faye stood virtually in his face.

"Please, Joshua, I don't want you to do this," she said as she grabbed his arm and pleaded with him. "I have a sickening feeling starting to eat in my stomach. You don't have to do this."

"Faye, seven children's lives are at stake," Joshua said in a heated voice. "Those pictures that I have of those little children, I can never get them out of my head. I see their faces and it makes me want to literally puke knowing that if I don't try to help get them set free, that will be on my conscience for the rest of my life. I have to go, Faye. I have to."

"But—"

Joshua's cellphone suddenly began to ring. He quickly yanked his phone out of his pocket and glared at the caller ID. It was his brother, Conrad.

"What is it, Conrad?" he said with venom in his voice when he answered the phone.

"What the hell did you write in your blog, man?" Conrad blasted over phone. "People everywhere are saying that all this mess that's happening in the streets across this country is because of you."

"Conrad, I'm in no mood to be talking about this with you on the phone," he said in a simmering tone. "I got other stuff on my mind."

"You've gone too damn far this time!" Conrad yelled in a

thunderous voice. "Anybody who causes all of this turmoil in the streets needs to be censored and thrown into jail! Who do you think you are to be writing something so divisive and disruptive? What the hell gives you the right to say anything you damn well please?"

"It's called freedom of speech!"

Joshua quickly hung up his phone. He looked back at Faye and saw her still glaring at him as if she wanted to handcuff him to the pole of their bed to keep him from going to St. Louis.

"Look, Faye, this is just something that I've got to do," he said forcefully. "I know you don't see this the way I see it, but—"

"No, I don't see it the way you see it," she said heatedly. "I think you're being foolish and reckless about this whole thing."

"Faye—"

The regal sound of their front doorbell suddenly rang. Both Joshua and Faye immediately gazed out of their bedroom toward the hallway as if someone were about to come up the staircase.

"Who in the world could that be at this hour?"

Joshua headed out of the bedroom and quickly descended the winding staircase. Still upset from arguing with Faye, he hurried through the vestibule and headed for the door. He immediately flipped on the porch light as he opened the front door. Through his locked storm door, he saw three men dressed in dark blue suits standing on his porch.

"Yes, may I help you?"

"We're from the Federal Bureau of Investigation," one of the men said as they all flipped out their wallets and showed their badges. "Mr. Edwards, we need to speak with you on an important matter."

Joshua gazed at the men suspiciously through the storm door for a few seconds, then finally unlocked the storm door and invited them in. He escorted them into the parlor as they all stared at Joshua.

"What's this all about?" Joshua finally said. He looked at all three men apprehensively.

"Mr. Edwards, we've attained knowledge that you're planning to board a flight to St. Louis tomorrow morning for the purpose of meeting with a contact member of Purification Of America Today. We can't allow you to go to this arranged meeting. For one, it could potentially be extremely dangerous, and two, it would interfere with our investigation to try to apprehend this criminal element."

Faye suddenly walked into the parlor. She slowly gazed warily around at the FBI men in the room.

"How do you know about my meeting in St. Louis tomorrow?" Joshua asked suspiciously as he suddenly glared at the FBI men.

"Because Purification Of America Today contacted you previously, we had to know if and when they would try to contact you again. So, since then, we've had you under surveillance."

"You've got my phones tapped?" Joshua asked in a heated voice.

"We've had to take measures to attain any information crucial in our investigation to apprehend and bring to justice the criminal element that's been committing these heinous crimes."

"There are laws against wiretapping!" Joshua yelled. "And I will sue the FBI and take legal action!"

"Mr. Edwards, let's not play games here," the agent said in a calm but forceful voice. "You're a civilian interfering with an investigation that concerns the federal government and national security. Now, we need you to step away from this and let our investigation take over."

"No, I can't do that," Joshua said as he firmly shook his head. "They specifically told me that if I didn't go through with what they wanted, they were going to kill those seven children. And I'm not about to have that on my conscience. I'm going tomorrow to St. Louis and I will be meeting with the contact person they'll be sending."

"Please, Joshua." Faye suddenly interrupted. "Why don't you listen to what these men—"

Joshua suddenly cut a hot glare at Faye and she immediately became silent.

"Mr. Edwards, we could very well detain you and bring you up on charges of interfering with a federal investigation."

"Then that's what you're going to have to do," Joshua said with a defiant look. "Because that'll be the only way you'll keep me from doing what I have to do."

The agent looked at Joshua for a long moment, then he suddenly whipped out his cellphone and made a call. For five long minutes, Joshua stood in his parlor listening to this FBI agent having an in-depth conversation with someone within the department of the Federal Bureau of Investigation. When the agent finally got off the phone, Joshua fully expected the FBI to handcuff him and haul him away.

"Mr. Edwards, I just got through talking to a couple of my superiors," the agent said as he peered hard into Joshua's eyes. "Since you insist on continuing to meet with this contact person, I've been instructed to tell you that you must wear a hidden wire to this prearranged meeting that our men will fit you with so that we'll constantly be able to monitor everything being said during the arranged meeting. Our men will be close by at a nearby location to monitor everything. And this is not negotiable."

Joshua slowly looked at his wife who stood silently at the entrance of the parlor, watching and listening to everything. He could see the sense of fear in her eyes as she stared back at him in muted silence. After a couple of seconds, Joshua slowly cut his eyes away from his wife and once again looked at the three FBI agents waiting for him to reply.

"Sure," he finally said in a low key voice. "That won't be a problem."

Chapter 10

Joshua arrived at the St. Louis airport the next morning off his flight from Los Angeles. When he stepped out of the airport, he suddenly remembered that today was his 48th birthday, but that didn't seem important considering what he was about to do.

As directed, he caught a cab outside the airport and went straight to a motel a block away from the intended meeting place, Kelsey's Soul Food Diner. When he arrived at the motel, he went to room 202 and knocked on the door. An FBI agent immediately opened the door and Joshua entered the room.

The motel room was packed. Room 202 had been turned into a control room with state of the art equipment everywhere for listening, eavesdropping, and surveillance. About ten FBI agents in the room immediately went to work getting Joshua ready for his interview. They ordered Joshua to strip from his business suit as they began applying wires all over his body and connecting tiny microphones to his bare chest. In fifteen minutes he was dressed and ready. They gave him a few last minute important instructions and sent him on his way.

A few minutes later, Joshua arrived in the parking lot of Kelsey's Soul Food Diner as he stepped out of the taxi and entered the diner. It was noon and the place was packed with lunchtime customers flooding into the diner to get something to eat before they headed back to work. Joshua, who looked like a busy businessman with a brief case clutched in his hand, ignored the long line of customers waiting in the buffet style line as he immediately began to scan the dining room. There was hardly a table empty. Most of the customers were black, with a few whites sprinkled here and there.

Figuring that the contact person he was supposed to meet would be white, Joshua slowly began to stroll through the dining area as he focused on the few white faces that populated the packed diner. He got a few stares from some of the customers who ate as he slowly approached them without a food tray in his hand, but he was quickly dismissed as he slowly sauntered by. Time was imperative to these diners who only had so much time for their lunch break, and no one seemed to want to waste a lot of time trying to figure out why some stranger was slowly creeping by without a food tray in his hand.

In the far back of the diner sitting at a small table in a corner was a white man eating all alone. Joshua slowly approached the man in the corner of the diner. The man looked to be in his mid-to-late fifties whose hair was beginning to gray. He wore sneakers, blue jeans, and a thick brown sweater zipped to his collar. The man looked to be thoroughly enjoying his meal and seemed to be without a care in the world. When Joshua slowly approached him, the man slowly looked up from his plate of food and gave Joshua a warm, enduring smile.

"Can I help you?" the man asked in a pleasant voice.

Joshua immediately felt embarrassed for interrupting this nice man's lunch. "I'm sorry to disturb you, sir. I was just looking for someone I was supposed to meet here at noon," he said in an apologetic voice. "My apologies, sir. I'll be—"

"Thomas Jefferson used to always eat lunch with his slaves," the man suddenly said as he continued smiling.

A cold shiver suddenly went down Joshua's back as he stared into the blue eyes of the man sitting at the table. The man had the warm face and radiant smile of an endearing, saintly pope who would forgive you of your sins and shower you with many blessings and good tithes. There was nothing ominous nor foreboding in this man's countenance; only good smiles and plenty of cheer.

"Please, have a seat," the man said as he continued to smile.

Joshua slowly looked around the packed dining area. No one seemed to be paying any attention to what took place at the table he stood at. Everyone was eating and minding his or her own business.

With a somewhat nervous hesitation, Joshua eased into the seat at the dining table where the man sat. He set his briefcase down next to him on the floor and slowly looked at the man sitting across from him.

The face of this man, as he continued to eat his lunch, wasn't one that seemed it would bomb Muslim mosques, blow up abortion clinics, kill atheists at a march on Washington, murder members of the Black Unity Coalition at a rally in Chicago, or kidnap seven innocent children from a daycare center in Detroit. He didn't even seem as though he could lead others of his brotherhood to commit atrocities or perpetrate violence on anyone. When Joshua, however, suddenly gazed at the back of the man's hand as he continued to eat his lunch, he instinctively knew that this man was a member of Purification Of America Today. The tattoo on the back of his hand of a hideous orange flaming skull with the initials P.O.A.T. above the unsightly skull was all the proof that Joshua needed.

"You're not eating?" the man said as he looked at Joshua with a smile.

Joshua once again took a quick look around the packed diner to determine could anyone hear their conversation, but once again, it appeared that no one in the diner could've cared less what went on at his table. The wires underneath Joshua's shirt suddenly began to brush against his chest, and Joshua wondered if the FBI was listening and recording everything being said at their table as they stated they would be doing. He had no doubt they were; this was home grown terrorism at its highest.

"No, I won't be eating," Joshua finally answered in a nervous voice.

"A little nervous?" the man said with a smile as he continued eating.

"Yes."

"I can tell."

"You're a member of Purfication Of America Today?" Joshua asked in a low voice so no one around them could hear their conversation. "Correct?"

"Mr. Edwards, you knew that when you sat down," the man said with a sly smile.

"Well, since you already know my name, do you mind telling me yours?"

"Thomas Paine."

"Another Founding Father of our country and the author of the pamphlet Common Sense published in 1776."

"That's very good, Mr. Edwards."

Joshua immediately noticed by the sound of the man's voice that he wasn't the one who'd been calling him previously. This was someone else, another member of Purification Of America Today.

"Sir, may I ask you a few questions?"

"You're going to ask me a good number of questions," the man said with a smile as he looked at Joshua. "You're going to interview me on our take concerning immigration and welfare in this country, remember?"

"Yes, I know that, but I have a few questions before we begin."

"Ask away."

"Why every time that I've been contacted, the person who's been calling me states his name as one of our founding presidents or Founding Fathers of our country, just as you did? What's the purpose of that?"

"We believe our Founding Fathers who did so much to establish this country need to be honored more reverently in this modern time," the man said as he continued eating. "The principals of this country were molded by their minds like the Constitution and the Bill of Rights. Now our Founding Fathers have virtually been forgotten and cast aside in this new time of ours, like so many other things that we used to enjoy in this country."

"They didn't mean for us to murder and bomb our fellow countrymen when we didn't agree with their views," Joshua suddenly said as he looked across the table at his lunch companion as his nervousness began to fade away.

The man slowly put his fork down in his plate and returned Joshua's stare. His charming, polite smile had disappeared.

"We're in a war, Mr. Edwards," he said in even voice. "Our values are being compromised every day by a corrupt system that has taken over this nation. And we, the brothers of Purification Of America Today, must address this issue before we forever lose this country. Now," he said as he peered hard into Joshua's eyes, "are there anymore questions before we begin?"

"Yes, I want to know if those kids who were kidnapped are actually and truly going to be released unharmed?"

"Of course they will," the man said as he suddenly wiped his mouth with a napkin after he'd finished cleaning his plate of his lunch. "Just as long as you do as you're told."

Joshua looked at the man across from him for a couple of seconds, then reached down and grabbed his briefcase from the floor. He opened the briefcase and pulled out a pen, a notepad with questions written on it that he'd already prepared for today's interview, and a small portable tape recorder. He laid the items on the table and began to prepare to start his interview.

"No recorder," the man suddenly said.

"What?"

"No recorder."

Joshua looked at the man for a second, then without putting up a fuss, quickly put the recorder back into his briefcase. Just a pen and notepad would be sufficient.

"Okay, sir," Joshua said as he looked down at his notes on his notepad. "What are the views that Purification Of America Today have concerning immigration?"

"This country is fast becoming a wasteland because it has let so many immigrants over the years, especially illegal immigrants, horde all of our resources and services. The vitality of this country is being drained daily because so many of these wetback illegal immigrants are receiving welfare benefits. The children they have who automatically become U.S. citizens have been a pipeline for these illegal families to sift billions and billions of dollars from the services that our country provides to them. We need to stop this humongous dam break that has taken place that's continuously flooding and drowning our country."

"How do you propose that should be done?"

"Mass deportations of all illegal immigrants at once should be the prime number one objective that this country should undertake immediately," the man said as he stared at Joshua with hard, steely eyes. "And if the government is unable to do it, then Purification Of America Today will wholeheartedly take upon this mission to eradicate this cancerous plague."

"What about the children who are born legally here in the United States from these parents?" Joshua asked as he returned his stare. "If their parents are detained and deported, the children will most likely have to be put in foster care here in the United States. Wouldn't mass deportation create a further problem by tearing these families apart and creating more of a burden for the government to deal with?"

"There would be no problem if every last child and parent were hauled out of this country and slung back across our border," the man said in a firm voice. "No citizenship should be granted to any child of an illegal immigrant. The rules are twisted and are in favor of the illegal, but Purification Of America Today plans to make everything smooth and right."

"And just how will Purification Of America Today plan to do that?"

"You shall soon see," he said as he suddenly began to break into a sly smile. "The revolution has finally begun."

Joshua gazed at his notes once again.

"Okay, welfare. What is your organization's take on it?"

"We believe it should totally be abolished."

"Totally?"

"It has turned this country into a socialist state where the government virtually takes care of all the needs that a citizen desires and wants like a little infant constantly crying for the suckle of its mother's breast to feed it continuously," he said with spite. "It restricts and retrains the empowerment of the individual. The individual ends up not relying on itself to provide for its own needs. The system, as it is now, offers a maze of programs to keep the individual perpetually locked into welfare where the individual eventually becomes addicted to it like a drug addict on the street who constantly needs a fix."

"You're trying to compare someone on welfare to a drug fiend?"

"Exactly," he said as he peered hard at Joshua. "The high that it gives the individual keeps the individual too intoxicated to see that there are other alternatives out there that are available to achieve what the individual needs and craves. It's a debilitating, suicidal system that needs to be abandoned so this country can stay afloat and survive before it totally sinks."

"Well, that's just insane," Joshua said in an incredulous voice. "Welfare is needed to provide for those who desperately need assistance and care who can't provide for themselves. It's an anchor for the poor in this country who struggle to survive and live every day, and who have been persecuted and oppressed throughout the years through no fault of their own."

"Like your people?"

"Yes, exactly," Joshua said in a resolute voice. "African Americans have especially been persecuted and oppressed throughout the years, and though there are a great deal of us who have striven to attain great things, some of us have been left behind to struggle and fight in a system that keeps persecuting and oppressing us. Until the playing field is leveled, there will always need to be a mechanism and a system in place to give those who are underprivileged a chance and an opportunity to succeed."

"A mechanism?" the man said incredulously.

"Yes."

"America wasn't formed to be a Marxist society that takes unduly from others and gives to those who may be in peril, Mr. Edwards," the man said harshly. "The climb up the ladder of achievement and success is one's own struggle to attain. Affirmative action, racial quotas, and government handouts to minorities violate the spirit that has made this country once great. Why, I'm sure more than half the people in here have probably benefited and gotten ahead of the line from such a corrupted, un-American movement that has now taken over this country as a free equal handout. Probably even you."

"I beg your pardon, sir," Joshua said in an annoyed voice. "But I've struggled many years to attain what I have, and I wasn't put or moved ahead of anyone's line. I worked hard every day to be in the position that I'm in today."

"Well, you just made my case," the man said as his sly smile returned. "This country is meant for those to pull up their own bootstraps and make their own way, and shouldn't be a communist welfare state to freely give away its resources to those who just want a free ride."

"But there are extenuating circumstances that have prevented many who are on welfare to overcome the obstacles that are in their lives," Joshua said in a combative voice. "There must and there always needs to be a system to help those in need. There will always be those who will be in need."

"America will no longer be a welfare state for those who continue to rob from this country," the man said as his smile vanished as a look of death suddenly took its place. "And Purification Of America Today will see to it that it happens. We have started the war for a new nation, Mr. Edwards, and we're not taking any prisoners."

Joshua stared into the eyes of the man sitting across from him as a shudder once again began to seize his body. The eyes of the man had suddenly become demented, like a switch had been flipped inside of him to something dark and ominous.

"Well, I believe we've covered enough here," Joshua finally said. He quickly collected his pen and notepad from the table as he stuffed them into his briefcase. "You will be getting my rebuttal to this interview, as you wish."

As Joshua was about to rise from the table, the man suddenly slid an envelope across to him.

"What's this?"

"It's for you, Mr. Edwards."

Joshua looked at the man suspiciously, then opened the envelope. The envelope contained a beautifully designed birthday card with the picture of a man on it. The man was surrounded by his entire family at a dinner table that contained a huge birthday cake with many lit candles. The man's family in the picture smiled joyously as they waited for the man to blow out the candles.

"What's the meaning of this?" Joshua asked in confusion as he looked at the man.

"Open the card, Mr. Edwards," the man said in a strange voice. "I believe you'll find what's inside very intriguing."

Joshua stared at the man for a few seconds as he gave him a puzzled look, then slowly opened the card. Inside the card was a written message:

Happy 48th birthday, Joshua Edwards. But if you want to live to see 49, then you better get out of here within ten seconds!

Confused and bewildered by the strange message on the birthday card, Joshua slowly looked up and couldn't believe his eyes. The man across from him had unzipped his brown sweater completely as he sat like a suicide bomber in his chair. He had on a vest strapped with enough dynamite and explosives to blow up the entire building demolition style. The man stared up at the ceiling with a lunatic-like smile as a small digital clock attached to his explosive vest was ticking down fast to zero.

"Oh, my God!" Joshua said in horror as he stared wide-eyed over at the man. "Oh, my God!"

Joshua quickly grabbed his briefcase and bolted from his chair.

"Everybody, get out of here!" he yelled frantically to everyone in the packed diner. "HE'S GOING TO BLOW UP THE PLACE! DAMNIT, GET OUT OF HERE!"

The people in the diner eating suddenly looked at Joshua as if he were crazy, but Joshua wasn't waiting around for another second. He stormed out of Kelsey's Soul Food Diner like a mad man.

Within seconds of storming out the diner, the entire building suddenly exploded as if a nuclear bomb had gone off. The powerful, massive explosion knocked Joshua hard to the pavement of the parking lot as smoke, dust, and debris went flying everywhere.

Dazed and rattled from the ruckus explosion, Joshua slowly tried to collect himself as he lay helplessly on the pavement of the parking lot.

When he finally gathered his wits, he slowly stared in utter horror at the burning carnage of what was left of the building. Only seconds ago, it was packed with a diner full of people.

That night after returning home from his flight back from St. Louis, Joshua was lying in bed staring at the ceiling in his bedroom with an ice pack on his head. The TV in the bedroom was on the national news. All over the news were constant reports on the suicide bombing that took place at the soul food diner in St. Louis that killed everyone inside the diner and the connection it had with Purification Of America Today. When news reports began to surface about the interview Joshua had conducted with the suicide bomber just seconds before the tragedy happened, Joshua's home phone began to ring off the hook. Reporters from everywhere desperately wanted to talk to him.

The tragic bombing, however, had virtually left Joshua in a conscious coma, and he wasn't taking any calls from anyone. As he lay staring at the ceiling with the ice pack on his head, he tried to cope with the realization that he'd been talking to the man who had planned to kill everyone inside the diner all along, and he, himself, was only seconds away from being one of the dead being reported on TV.

Faye, who stood by his bedside, did whatever she could to try to comfort him. She answered the endless phone calls that came from reporters all across the country, continuously telling them that her husband couldn't talk at the moment. Eventually, she just turned off all the phones in the house so Joshua could get some peace and rest.

"You want anything to eat or drink?" she said in a concerned voice as she stood by his bedside, staring compassionately down at him as he rested. "I can fix you some soup and make you a sandwich. Maybe it'll help a little if you get something on your stomach."

"Nothing is going to help take away the nightmare of seeing that place explode like it did," Joshua said barely above a whisper as he continued to stare at the ceiling like a zombie. "All of those people, Faye." He slowly began to shake his head. "All of them just gone in a split second."

"I was afraid something terrible like this was going to happen," Faye said. "I never wanted you to go to St. Louis and meet with that person. It just didn't sound right."

"Yeah," Joshua said in a solemn, grave voice. "I guess you were right all along."

"Well, from what you told me, you did all that you could," she said in a comforting voice. "There was simply nothing that you could do to save those people in that diner."

"This Purification Of America Today," Joshua said in a hollow voice as he stared at the ceiling. "They have to be brought down before they destroy or kill anyone else. They have to."

"That's what the FBI and other law enforcement agencies around the country are trying desperately to do. They're working around the clock to accomplish just that."

"But will anyone else be killed by this organization's wretched, evil hands before they can do it?" Joshua said in a languid voice. "That's the question."

"Well, I believe I'll go on downstairs and fix you that soup and sandwich," Faye said in a compassionate voice. "I believe it'll help a little to calm your nerves."

When Faye left the bedroom, Joshua continued staring at the ceiling with the ice pack on his head. The coolness of the ice slowly began to relieve the stress and tension he was under. It was like a fire hose melting the fire that had been burning in his head since he saw Kelsey's Soul Food Diner erupt into flames.

An hour later after starting to feel a little better, Joshua removed the ice pack from his head and sat up in bed. With the TV on mute as the news still focused on the suicide bombing that took place in St. Louis, Joshua reached into his pocket and pulled out the pictures of the seven kidnapped kids that he constantly kept with him. He began to stare at each individual picture.

These individual pictures were the entire reason he'd gone to St. Louis in the first place. Even though Joshua had just gone through the worst experience of his life, he still wanted to secure the freedom of these innocent little children's lives. Joshua knew the only way that he could potentially get this kidnapped group of children freed from their captors and returned to their mothers, was to do the interview that Purification Of America Today wanted him to do.

Purification Of America Today had promised that if he met with the contact person they sent and he did some sort of rebuttal to the interview in his blog, they would release a captured child. With the hellish evil event that happened today literally still smoldering, Joshua seriously had his doubts about that. However, if by some remote chance Purification Of America Today kept their word and actually released a child after he wrote his rebuttal, then Joshua couldn't afford not to do his part. An innocent child's life was at stake, and Joshua was going to do everything in his power to see to it that every child had a chance to be freed.

Feeling somewhat rejuvenated and now focused on the task at hand, Joshua rose from bed as he went to his closet and grabbed his briefcase. He pulled out his laptop from his briefcase and sat back on the bed.

Joshua switched on his laptop, clicked on the Internet, and logged into his blog. Going to a new entry page, he entitled his new blog, My Rebuttal To Today's Incendiary Event. It almost pained him to be used as a pawn in Purification Of America Today's wicked evil games, but still the mission had to be accomplished. A child had to be freed:

My Rebuttal To Today's Incendiary Event

I was contacted by a member of Purification Of America Today to do an interview concerning the state of immigration and welfare in this country for a child, which this organization has kidnapped, to be released unharmed. This is my rebuttal to that interview.

Purification Of America Today states that all illegal immigrants should be immediately deported, that they are draining our country's resources and have become a burden on American society. While this position cannot be totally admonished, there are other extenuating circumstances that need to be accounted for.

Many children of illegal immigrants have been born here in the United States and have automatically become U.S. citizens. To deport their parents would mean that these children would become orphans here in America and would have to be placed in foster care. This would cause a further burden on our foster care system here in America. Also, the aspect of tearing apart thousands of families would create another major problem that would simply be too hard to remedy.

There needs to be another solution to this urgent national problem. Illegal immigration is a problem for this country, but mass deportations would create untold problems not only on the foster care system in this country, but for the children of illegal immigrants who are deported.

Purification Of America Today also stated that the welfare system in this country needs to be totally abolished because it has created a perpetuity of endless recipients who constantly abuse the system.

Welfare provides an essential element of many people's daily lives for those who struggle to provide the necessities required for a normal standard of living. Everyone in America, who is able, should strive to gain meaningful employment that will provide for their everyday basic needs, but there are circumstances that prevent some citizens from attaining employment to achieve this basic purpose.

People who have disabilities and those who have been deemed not employable for various reasons are often in need of services to help their daily standard of living. Also, systematic road blocks throughout the history of this country have prevented some segments of society to fully achieve the American dream and have thus left them in a disadvantaged state. To completely deny these disadvantaged groups without the means of getting the basic necessities of life would be a terrible injustice.

Welfare is needed. There may need to be a closer examination of how the system as a whole can become more financially prudent, but never should it be entirely abolished.

This is my rebuttal statement to the interview conducted between myself and a member of Purification Of America Today.

When Joshua finished the blog and sent it off, he wondered would a kidnapped child be released as promised. But while Joshua sat in his bed and began to stare at the muted widescreen TV, he wondered what would truly be accomplished if that were to happen. He truly began to wonder if one freed little child would somehow equate to all the lives tragically lost in Kelsey's Soul Food Diner earlier today.

Chapter 11

The next morning Joshua woke up from an uneasy night of sleep as he reached for the remote on the nightstand next to him and turned on the news. The first thing he saw was the breaking news report.

One of the kidnapped kids who had been taken from the Detroit daycare center, a four-year-old black girl named China Rutledge, was found early this morning at a Philadelphia bus station. She was in good health, but terrified. Apparently she'd been dropped off at the front entrance of the bus station. Witnesses saw a green van pull up to the bus station around 3 a.m., dropped the four-year-old girl off, and sped away. A Massachusetts license plate was reported seen on the green van, but nothing further was reported.

Joshua couldn't believe what he heard. Purification Of America Today, the lowest forms of devils, had actually kept their word and had released a child unharmed. A relief suddenly came over Joshua like he'd never felt before, but his mood quickly tempered. He suddenly realized there were still six innocent little children still being held against their will.

His mood grew even darker when the news not only recaptured the horror of yesterday's suicidal bombing in St. Louis that claimed the lives of thirty-seven people, but they began to show all the turmoil, fighting, and rioting still going on in the streets.

Every news channel that Joshua flipped to on his remote, he was being criticized and lambasted by the media for the inflammatory blog he wrote that started all the upheaval in the streets of America. However, Joshua was stunned beyond belief when he suddenly turned to one of the channels and saw his brother, Conrad, on one of the major networks. His own brother was criticizing and attacking him with a vengeance like he'd never seen before.

Joshua just stared at the TV with his mouth wide open in disbelief. His dear older brother had finally made the big time, and he was using the spotlight to shred his younger brother to pieces.

Still shaken up over what happened yesterday and feeling down at what was going on in the streets across America, Joshua decided to take a quick shower, get dressed, and head to Sam's Rib Shack. He needed to get out of the house for awhile and congregate with some normal, law-abiding folk; people who weren't trying to blow him to smithereens or get him to do some twisted interview to get innocent children released. He just needed to talk to a friendly face, and Big Sam was as friendly as they came.

When Joshua finally arrived at Sam's Rib Shack in Crenshaw and entered the joint, he found the place virtually empty of any customers. Only one lone customer sat at the bar sipping on a beer. The stereo, which normally pumped out seventies R&B music all around the restaurant, wasn't on and neither was the huge widescreen TV in the corner playing. Silence virtually reigned over the entire place. Joshua knew it was a little early for the normal crowd who usually frequented Sam's Rib Shack to be in attendance, but that was fine with him. He just needed a friendly face or two to communicate with to lift his spirits.

Joshua gave a respectful nod to the gentleman sitting alone at the bar drinking a beer as he also had a seat. He slowly looked around the empty place and noticed that the chairs had yet to be taken down from the tables. The place was still in the mode of closed for the night.

"Big Sam around?" Joshua said to the older gentleman drinking his beer.

"He's in the back taking care of some stuff," the gentleman said as he suddenly gave Joshua a precarious look. "Man, you're a fortunate one. You know that?"

"Pardon?"

"I saw on the news last night how that diner exploded in St. Louis. They said you were in there interviewing some cat from that Purification Of America Today organization when you ran out of there seconds before it exploded. Is that really true?"

"Yeah," Joshua said. He slowly closed his eyes as the nightmare suddenly came back to life. "Unfortunately, it's true."

"Man, ain't no way I could be sitting in here like you're doing right now," the man said with a chuckle as he shook his head. "I think I'd be done checked into a mental ward getting some treatment after going through something like that."

"I think I might just do that," Joshua said with a deep sigh. "Because it certainly feels like I need it."

Big Sam suddenly came out of his office and entered the bar area. The six-foot-six man, who was built like a grizzly bear, had a stunned look as he glanced at Joshua. It seemed he was totally shocked to see Joshua sitting at his bar today.

"Josh, my man," Big Sam said in a concerned voice. He came over and rested his elbows on the bar and peered hard at Joshua. "Man, are you alright? I heard what happened yesterday at that restaurant in St. Louis."

"Hell, the whole world has heard about it," the man next to Joshua said as he let out another chuckle.

"I'm alright," Joshua said as he tried to give a slight smile. "Just a little worn out."

"Well, Linda and my other two cooks haven't arrived yet to fix anything to eat, but you want anything to drink? You want some coffee, a Coke, Sprite—"

"Give me a tall beer, like the gentleman next to me."

"A beer," Big Sam said as he gave Joshua a confused look. "You're jumping off the wagon?"

"Yep, today I am," Joshua said. "I need something a little stronger than a Sprite."

Big Sam poured Joshua a tall glass of draft beer. Joshua took the beer and nearly drained it in one gulp.

"Tough morning, huh?"

"It's been a tough morning, tough night, tough past two days, tough past two weeks," Joshua said as he looked at Big Sam and shook his head. "I've been through some tough stuff in my lifetime, but not this crazy. I had to deal with what happened yesterday, and now all over America there's rioting and unrest in the streets that I'm being blamed for. Yeah, it's been pretty tough."

"That was some pretty crazy stuff what that suicide bomber did killing all those people like that," Big Sam said as he looked at Joshua with sympathy. "That must've been one horrible experience. Hell, I served in Vietnam fighting in the toughest hell holes there were and never came close to anything that you just went through."

"I tell you, I swear, I didn't see it coming," Joshua said as he drank the rest of his beer. Big Sam quickly refilled his glass with another round. "I was contacted by someone from Purification Of America Today a couple of days ago to do an interview with one of their members on immigration and welfare in America. They said they'd release a kidnapped child if I wrote a rebuttal to their interview in my blog.

"Well, when I arrived at the meeting place, the diner in St. Louis, the contact member from Purification Of America Today was already there eating lunch like any other customer," Joshua said as he continued. "He looked like some harmless middle age white dude wearing a brown sweater and blue jeans. We did the interview and all, and everything seemed okay, but at the very end, he hands me this birthday card."

"A birthday card?"

"Yeah, somehow he already knew that yesterday was my birthday."

"Damn, I didn't know yesterday was your birthday."

"Hell, I'd almost forgotten it until he slides me this crazy birthday card."

"What did the card say?"

"It said happy 48th birthday. But if I wanted to live to see 49, then I better get the hell out of there in ten seconds. Next thing I know, the guy had unzipped his brown sweater and was revealing a bomb vest with all sorts of dynamite and explosives attached to it with a digital clock that was ticking down fast. It startled me beyond comprehension. I got up, yelling for everyone to get out, then I shot out of there faster than a world class sprinter. Next thing I know, the place exploded."

"Why was the interview taking place in St. Louis at a soul food diner?"

"That's where they wanted me to meet the contact person they were sending for me to interview," Joshua said as confounded as Big Sam and the gentleman next to him were staring at him. "They obviously had already planned to kill a lot of black people in the first place. That's the only reason I can figure why they wanted me to meet at this soul food restaurant. Why St. Louis, I have no idea. I was totally shocked this morning when I heard that they'd even released one of the kidnapped children unharmed."

"If you ask me, those Purification Of America Today people are as wile as a fox and as evil as the devil," the man next to him said while he shook his head. "I wouldn't go within a hundred feet of any of them."

"You can say that again," Joshua said, glancing across at his drinking partner. "The FBI told me last night after the incident that under no circumstances was I to meet with any other member of their organization if I were contacted again, but they didn't have to tell me that. Ain't no way I'm going within a hundred miles of anyone connected with them again, no matter who they promise to release."

Two hours later, Joshua was still sitting at the bar gabbing away with Big Sam. The gentleman next to him had already paid for his beer and had left, but the place began to come alive as other patrons slowly flooded in.

Joshua had just finished his sixth beer. The tension he was under when he first entered the establishment had now somewhat faded. Big Sam was about to pour him his seventh beer, but Joshua suddenly held up his hand like a traffic cop halting traffic. He already felt pretty good and he knew he'd had enough.

"You going to be alright driving home, Josh?" Big Sam asked like a good, concerned friend.

"I'm fine, Big Sam," Joshua said as he reached into his wallet and laid the tab fee for his drinks on the bar. "My old psychiatrist might not approve, but I'm fine."

Big Sam quickly shoved the money back. "It's on the house, Josh. You've been through enough. We're just two old friends sitting around talking and having a beer."

"You never stop amazing me, Big Sam," Joshua said with a smile. "I don't even know why I still go to see Dr. Mitchell. It's you I should be throwing all my business to."

"How's the wife and two kids?"

"Oh, they're doing—"

"Say, Big Sam," one of the cooks suddenly yelled as he interrupted their conversation. "Someone is on the phone wanting to speak with you."

Big Sam went into his office to take the call. Joshua sat at the bar and drank what was left of his final beer. He pulled out a twenty and laid it on the bar as he prepared to leave. No matter what Big Sam said, he wanted to pay him something. If Big Sam didn't want payment for the beers, he could consider the twenty a tip.

"Hey, Josh, you got somebody calling you from the downtown jail," Big Sam said when he suddenly came out of his office and handed Joshua the phone.

"From jail?"

"Yep, and don't worry, it's not your son."

Big Sam went out in the dining area to take care of some business. Joshua slowly pulled the phone to his ear. He hesitated answering, fearing something bad.

"Hello?" he answered with reservation.

"You don't know me, but I have some valuable information that I think you want to hear."

"Who is this?"

"Just call me Mr. Z."

"Alright, *Mr. Z*," Joshua said in a flippant voice. "How did you know where to reach me, and why are you calling me from jail?"

"To answer your first question, word gets around. To answer your second question, because this has been my home for the past six months," the deep voice of the man said. "The reason I'm calling is I got information on where those kids are located, and that's not all I can tell you. I can tell you a whole lot more."

"A whole lot more of what?"

"About Purification Of America Today."

"And you can be some damn crazy crackpot calling me."

"Can a crackpot know that someone from Purification Of America Today called you around midnight the Saturday of the initial attacks and told you he was George Washington? Can a crackpot know how the voice sounded of the person who called you? Didn't it sound like the raspy voice of an old man?"

Joshua remained silent as he held the phone to his ear.

"Come down to the jail and ask for Mr. Z," the man finally said in a confident voice, "and we'll talk further."

When the call ended, Joshua held the phone limp in his hand. For the longest he sat silently at the bar, debating whether he should go down to the jail to meet this unexpected caller.

Against his better judgment, Joshua arrived at the downtown Los Angeles jail an hour after he'd finished talking to the caller who'd just phoned Sam's Rib Shack. After entering the building, Joshua checked in at the information desk and asked to see Mr. Z after giving the clerk his own name.

Joshua fully expected the busy clerk to give him a bizarre look after making such an odd, strange request, but the clerk merely pecked into his computer a few strokes and told Joshua the inmate, Mr. Z, would be able for visitation in twenty minutes. No further information was required. With hundreds of inmates constantly being booked and entered into the system of a big city jail daily, an odd name here and there was probably not uncommon.

Joshua entered the overcrowded visitation room and began to scan his surroundings. He immediately noticed a long thick glass window that separated the inmates from the visitors. Red colored phones were stationed at each individual section along a long table connected to the glass wall for communication with the inmates. After thoroughly scanning his surroundings, Joshua sat at the far end of the visitation room. He waited patiently for the inmate he'd come to see to enter on the prisoner side.

The visitation room was a virtual beehive with all types of conversations going on in various languages. There was English being spoken, Spanish, French, Chinese, Russian, Arabic, and many other languages being blabbered all at once. To add to the linguistic mess, babies were crying, children were restless and playing, and spouses of several inmates were either sobbing because their mates were locked up and away from them, or they were ranting and yelling for money needed to pay bills. The place was literally a zoo, and after a few minutes of idle waiting, Joshua seriously thought about just getting up and leaving this crazy, insane place.

Twenty minutes later, a huge white inmate in an orange prison suit suddenly entered the visitation room on the inmate side. Right off, Joshua knew it had to be Mr. Z. He looked like a biker from some prehistoric time who probably rode on wheels made of stone. His hair was wild and mangy, and it draped all down his back well below his posterior. He had a huge tattoo engraved on his forehead that simply said KILL NIGGERS!

The inmate, glancing carefully at the faces of the visitors sitting on the other side of the glass partition, finally made his way down to the end of the visitation room and had a seat across from Joshua. He stared through the glass window at Joshua like a huge, angry lineman sizing up the quarterback of an opposing team. Once the football was snapped, he was probably going to tear through the line and eat the QB for lunch.

Joshua, unnerved by this huge inmate's threatening demeanor, picked up the red phone on his side as the inmate picked up the phone on his. The two stared at each other in total silence while they both held the phones to their mouths.

"Well?" Joshua finally said when the silence began to go on too long.

"I can help you," the man said as he glared at Joshua.

"Is that a fact?"

"Yes, that's a fact."

Joshua suddenly looked across the glass partition and noticed a tattoo on the hand of the inmate. The initials P.O.A.T. were engraved on his hand, the exact same as the contact person at that soul food diner in St. Louis.

"And exactly why would you want to help me?" Joshua said when he glanced at the tattoo engraved on the inmate's forehead. "It doesn't appear to me that you're very fond of my particular skin color or any of my people."

"Let's just say I don't agree with what Purification Of America Today has been doing lately," he said in a cool voice. "Plus being locked up in here with everybody up under the sun, you start to see things differently."

"So, you're saying you've reformed?" Joshua asked in a cynical tone.

"No, I still have my beliefs," he answered with tooth and nail. "But I believe there are ways of attaining them other than cold, bloodied murder."

Joshua stared at the hardened inmate across the glass partition for the longest. He didn't know what to make of the tattooed brute he stared at, but he was willing to listen to what he had to offer.

"Okay, how can you help?"

"You need to know how our organization works."

"How long have you been a member?"

"For over ten years, and I've seen everything there is to know," he said as his stare peered through the glass partition like a red hot beam. "We started out like a small clan who was fed up with the counterculture movement that was beginning to sweep across this country. The gay rights, the illegal immigrants flooding in, the gun control advocates, Muslims taking over the country, affirmative action stripping the white man down, abortion freaks popping up everywhere, the government invading in on our rights, and a whole host of other treacherous plagues that were beginning to stain our country made us boiling mad. We began to organize and recruit others who thought as we did, who wanted to eradicate the element that was beginning to destroy this nation.

"So we began to grow in numbers and strength," he said as he continued. "Within a few years, we had grown to over a hundred good loyal brothers. Now we have over a thousand members with chapters in several states across the country."

"How many chapters are there?"

"They're twelve in all. There's one in Iowa, Montana, Texas, Washington, two in Idaho, two in Oklahoma, and four here in California. The structure is fairly basic. Each chapter has an executive over each chapter."

"Like a grand dragon or grand wizard?"

"We're not the Ku Klux Klan, Mr. Edwards," he suddenly said with spite. "Our philosophy is much different from theirs. Plus we're far more effective in our tactics."

"I can certainly believe that," Joshua said as he continued to stare at the inmate across from him.

"The supreme executor of our entire organization is Bob Kramer. He's eighty-six and he's hell bent on purifying America of all of what afflicts this country before his dying day comes."

"He talks with a raspy voice?"

"That's the one," he said with a nod. "He's the one who's been calling you and has given you the opportunity to state your case in your blog, Justice For All. He's thoroughly studied and followed your editorial critiques for the past year and thinks you're a worthy adversary."

"I'm touched," Joshua said in a sarcastic tone. "Okay, you've given me a history of your wonderful organization, why your organization is doing what it's doing, and how the structural command of your organization works. Now, where are the kidnapped children?"

"Who was the last Founding Father you heard someone from Purification Of America Today mentioned to you?"

"I don't know," Joshua said in an irritated voice as he shrugged. "What the hell difference does that matter?"

"There are usually hidden meanings behind each name that our organization uses whenever it states one of those Founding Fathers," the inmate said. "You must know the complete history of each Founding Father, and it will more than likely tell you an important clue whenever that name is stated."

"Wait a minute," Joshua said as he desperately tried to backtrack to when he last remembered hearing one of the Founding Fathers mentioned. "If I remember correctly, the guy I met at that soul food restaurant in St. Louis mentioned one of those Founding Fathers to me when I first approached him. He said something to the effect that Thomas Jefferson liked to eat lunch with his slaves."

Joshua pulled out his smartphone and quickly googled Thomas Jefferson's name.

"Okay, it says here that Thomas Jefferson was an American Founding Father and the principal author of the Declaration of Independence," Joshua said as he began to read Thomas Jefferson's bio when he found it. "He was elected the third president of the United States. Primarily of English ancestry, Thomas Jefferson was born and educated in Virginia—"

"Bingo," the inmate suddenly said while he stared across the glass partition at Joshua.

"You're telling me those kidnapped kids have been taken to Virginia?" Joshua said as he eyed the inmate. "But where in Virginia?"

"You tell me."

Joshua read more of Thomas Jefferson's bio that he'd googled on his phone. "It goes on to say Thomas Jefferson inherited from his father 5,000 acres of land, including Monticello. Monticello was the primary plantation of Thomas Jefferson. He used slaves to cultivate tobacco and other mixed crops on the plantation located just outside Charlottesville, Virginia."

"Well . . . well," the inmate suddenly said with a sinister chuckle. "I guess I'm looking at the black Sherlock Holmes over here."

"Well, I guess there's no way on earth that they can be held on some public historical plantation," Joshua said rhetorically. "So I guess what you're saying is they're being held somewhere around Charlottesville, Virginia."

The inmate remained silent while he stared at his guest.

"So, why should I believe what you just told me is true?" Joshua asked in a skeptical voice.

"There's no reason not to believe it."

"And why are you betraying your organization's secrets to me?"

"I told you," he said with steely eyes. "I don't agree with the method of how our organization is going about trying to execute our objectives."

"And why tell me?" he asked with skepticism. "Why not tell the FBI or some other law agency in this country? They would certainly be more equipped to handle this grave situation."

"I don't trust the government anymore," he said with bitterness as he stared at Joshua. "Or maybe just this once, Mr. Edwards, I believe in affirmative action."

The inmate hung up the phone and rose from his seat. He immediately departed from his side of the crowded visitation room.

Chapter 12

After leaving the jail, Joshua rushed straight to the Federal Bureau of Investigations' division office in Los Angeles. He met with a couple of agents and conveyed everything that Mr. Z had told him during his jail visit.

Joshua relayed all the pertinent background disclosed to him about the history of Purification Of America Today; the information about Bob Kramer, their eighty-six-year old executive leader; the information about the hidden meanings behind the Founding Fathers; and the information about all the different chapters that Purification Of America Today had in operation in the states of Iowa, Montana, Texas, Washington, Idaho, Oklahoma, and California. More important, Joshua relayed what he was told during his jail visit about Virginia being potentially the location where the six remaining kidnapped kids were being held.

Within two hours, Joshua had painstakingly relayed every little detail he could remember to the FBI about his jail visitation. When he'd finally finished divulging everything, Joshua felt like a postman who had dumped all of his daily route mail onto the FBI's desk. He desperately wanted nothing left untold, because he truly hoped it would lead to the rescue of those six precious kids. Even more important, he hoped it would lead to the dismantling, once and for all, of this evil, wretched extremist hate group terrorizing the country.

Chapter 13

That Sunday, Joshua and Faye once again hosted Sunday dinner for the family. Conrad and Lacy, quite naturally, weren't invited to this particular Sunday afternoon dinner considering the animosity that Joshua and his older brother had gotten into toward the end of the last dinner, but Kahila and Tyesha, along with her newly married partner, Patricia, were coming over today.

Joshua, even after being counseled by his psychiatrist, was still a little uneasy about meeting Patricia for the first time. He didn't care one bit that she was white; it was just the fact that Tyesha had actually gone ahead and had finally done it. After years of dabbling around and being romantically involved with several females, Tyesha had actually solidified what she'd always said she'd do. She had legally married someone from the same sex, and Joshua, deep down, still couldn't adjust to it.

When all the guests finally arrived for the 3 p.m. dinner and were sitting around the dining table, the dinner got off to a fairly good start. The menu of roast beef, baked potato, Caesar salad, bread, and red wine seemed to be to everyone's satisfaction.

Joshua purposely didn't bring up the subject of Tyesha's marriage, so as not to start an uncomfortable dialogue that could lead to an awkward confrontation. He hoped that Faye and Kahila, or Tyesha and Patricia for that matter, wouldn't bring up the topic of their marriage so he wouldn't have to confront what tore at his soul. For the moment, however, it didn't seem he had to worry about any of that. The subject of Purification Of America Today dominated the conversation around the table.

"Damn, for one time I actually agreed with what you had to say in your blog, Pops," Kahila said with a half-filled wine glass in his hand as he looked at his father at the head of the table.

Today Kahila was dressed in all black like a bona fide Black Panther member as the red wine seemed to super fuel his engine. He rambled and blabbered nonstop about everything he could think of.

"We needed to take to the streets and protest what this scourge of a racist organization, Purification Of America Today, has been doing lately, particularly to black people," he said with hostility. "The Black Unity Coalition, from city to city, has been fighting these cousins and relatives of this racist organization who want to uphold and spread their racist views. You were right, Dad. Just like you said in your blog that you titled A Treacherous Evil That Needs Resolving, we will fear no more. It's time for us to stand up and fight the oppressor. It's time for an eye for an eye and a tooth for a tooth. And that's just what the hell we're doing, too," he said with even more hostility in his voice. "We're giving them bastards an eye for eye and a tooth for a tooth out there in them streets."

"Kahila, watch your mouth!" Faye said with a heated glare. She suddenly looked at her new daughter-in-law sitting next to Tyesha as she showed her an apologetic face. "We don't need that kind of vain talk at this dinner table."

"Sorry, Ma," Kahila said as he drank the rest of his wine. "But we're in a war, and sometimes in war all hell comes out."

"Has the Black Unity Coalition been tussling with other racist groups out in the streets here in L.A.?" Tyesha suddenly asked her brother. "Have y'all been in a lot of confrontations here like they've been saying on the news that's been happening elsewhere around the country?"

"Damn right we have, little Sis," Kahila said full of bravado as he refilled his wine glass. "We've been tussling with the Skin Heads, White Power Front, Aryan Nation, The Hell Saints, and a whole bunch of other racist hate groups that have clashed with us out in them streets. We show them what the Black Unity Coalition is all about. We're strong black brothers and sisters who are tired of taking all the crap that the system has thrown down our throats. We want justice, and damnit, we want it right now."

"Kahila, please don't get yourself into any trouble out in them streets," Faye said with deep concern. "It's dangerous out there right now, and you need to show some common sense and restraint. What happened in Chicago with those people getting killed should give you pause to count your blessings that you're still here."

"Ma, these are dangerous times," he said in a firm voice. "We have to stand and fight against bigotry and oppression by any means necessary."

"Son, I didn't write that blog to start a war in the streets," Joshua said as he glared at Kahila. "I may have misspoken a little because I was so upset after those kids were kidnapped from that daycare center in Detroit, but I didn't intend for violence to erupt in the streets. Violence confronted by violence will never solve anything. It'll only lead to nothing but death."

"Well, sometimes you have to stand and fight and not worry about the outcome when you're faced with a threat that must be defeated."

"Kahila, you've been in enough trouble as it is," Joshua said as he lashed out. "You don't need anything else to go on your record."

"The hell with my record!" Kahila said as he beamed a hot look at his father. "We're in a war, and I'm going to stand and fight with my brothers and sisters of the Black Unity Coalition for what needs to be fought for."

Joshua slowly lowered his head and let out a deep sigh. He knew his son was as militant as a stubborn mule when it came to confronting anything that he deemed an injustice. Kahila had been a member of the Black Unity Coalition for three years and had been in several scrapes and altercations over the years. Joshua knew his son had a propensity for violent behavior and would fight literally anyone at the drop of a dime.

Feeling a little uneasy, Joshua slowly looked at his wife at the other side of the table, and he could see the deep concern in her eyes for their son. They seemed to both know that their son was a ticking bomb ready to go off at any moment.

"Mr. Edwards, what was it like being in that restaurant in St. Louis interviewing that member from Purification Of America today?" Patricia suddenly asked Joshua, breaking the brief silence at the table. "That must've been some experience."

Joshua, and everyone else, suddenly looked at Patricia. The new addition to their inner family circle hadn't said much since the dinner had begun. In fact, Joshua had somewhat mentally put Patricia to the side as Kahila rambled on and on about the Black Unity Coalition and their scrapes with all the hate groups that they'd encountered in the streets.

In a flash, however, Joshua had totally put his son's predicament out of his mind as he glanced at Patricia. Seeing Tyesha's wedded mate sitting next to her all of a sudden brought the issue of what he'd been internally dealing with back into focus, and what he was dealing with stared him right square in the face.

"Oh, please, enough with the formalities," he said with a charming smile. "Call me Joshua. And it was quite an audacious experience."

"That must've been horrible seeing that building explode knowing all those people had just been killed."

"Absolutely," Joshua said with a somber face. "I've had nightmares about that ever since. For the life of me, I didn't see it coming when I was interviewing the guy. The man was a racist, that's for sure. But at the moment when I was interviewing him inside that soul food restaurant with all those people sitting around eating, he didn't seem much of a threat. Who knew he'd be strapped with all those explosives underneath that brown sweater he was wearing."

"It's not your fault that those people were killed like that," Patricia said in a heartwarming voice. "You were only trying to get all of those innocent little children freed and returned to their mothers. I thought what you did was mighty brave and commendable."

"Thank you, Patricia," Joshua said with a nod and a smile. "That was mighty commendable on your part to say."

"That's just like my baby," Tyesha said with a smile. She began to stroke Patricia's long blonde hair. "She's always thinking of others and offering love to those in need. That's what makes her so special."

Tyesha and Patricia suddenly engaged in a little kiss at the table. The show of affection wasn't much, but Joshua suddenly began to frown as if the roast beef he'd just eaten had soured in his stomach.

Joshua slowly gazed across the dining table at Faye. She stared back at him with hooded eyes as if to say please don't start any trouble. Joshua then glanced at Kahila at the table, but knew his son didn't care one iota what went on. His son was busy refilling more wine and draining the contents in his glass like a drunken sailor who'd just hit the first bar when he came ashore.

"So, I know Tyesha has spoken about you several times," Joshua said as he carefully phrased his words, "but where did you two meet, Patricia?"

"We met about two years ago during one of our first meetings when we were just starting to plan and formulate our Internet blog, New Day."

"New Day?"

"That's the name of our blog site that we promote LGBT issues to all of our followers around the country," Tyesha said with a huff. "Damn, Daddy, I thought you knew about New Day a long time ago. We have nearly a hundred thousand followers to our blog. It may not be some award winning blog like Justice For All that has millions of followers, but we do quite well. You ain't the only one around here who has the pulse of what's happening in America."

"That's telling him, little Sis," Kahila suddenly said as he let out a drunken chuckle.

"Ah, New Day. The LGBT blog. Yes, of course," Joshua said in an apologetic voice. He once again focused his attention back on Patricia. "So, Patricia, what are you and Tyesha's plans for the future?"

"Well, we intend to devote a tremendous amount of time and effort in expanding New Day over the next several years. We want the LGBT community to prosper and grow and have full equality in this country," she said with a thoughtful smile. "And, let's see, we plan on maybe doing some traveling abroad in a few years, and we also plan on adopting two or three children into our family to raise and love."

"Adopting children?"

"Yes, sir."

Joshua slowly looked at his wife with wary eyes as Faye quickly interjected into the conversation.

"Well, that certainly sounds like a promising future," Faye said with a kind smile. "I certainly hope the best for you two. I can see that Tyesha certainly picked a lovely, warmhearted, and intelligent mate to spend her life with. And we're certainly glad that you're a member of our family now."

"Thank you, Mrs. Edwards."

"Now, what did my husband just tell you?" Faye said with a bright smile. "Family members around here are on first name basis, and you're family now."

"Sorry," Patricia said as she returned Faye's bright smile. "I'll remember that from now on."

Faye slowly looked back across the dining table at Joshua as she still smiled, but Joshua wasn't smiling one bit. He still had a somewhat perturbed look as he stared at Tyesha and Patricia.

"So, you two are really planning on adopting kids?"

"Yes, sir," Patricia said as she continued smiling. "Maybe not right off, but somewhere down the road. Maybe in two or three years we'll adopt."

"Joshua, you ready for a little dessert now?" Faye suddenly said with a wary smile. "Why don't you get the chocolate cake from the kitchen and serve us dessert."

"Not now, Faye."

"But I'm sure everyone is ready for some dessert by now. We've all finished our dinner and I know everyone is—"

"Not now, Faye," he said as he gave his wife a stern look. He slowly gazed back across the table at Tyesha and Patricia. "Well, I'm sure you two will seriously think long and hard about adopting any children before you two go through the process of adoption," he said politely. "Won't you?"

"What's there to think about?" Tyesha said with a quick tongue. "If we want to adopt, then we'll adopt."

"Tyesha, raising children takes proper guidance and care. A child must be raised in an environment where the child's state of mind won't be unduly influenced or swayed by somewhat egregious factors."

"What the hell you talking about, somewhat egregious factors?"

"Joshua, let's just drop this and have some dessert—"

"I'm talking about a child being raised in a home with a father and a mother," Joshua said directly to the point as he quickly cut Faye off. "If you intend to adopt a child, how are you going to raise the child in your home?"

"You mean are we going to raise the child to be straight or gay?"

"Quite frankly, yes," Joshua said as he peered hard at his daughter. "How will this child be raised in this type of a home?"

"Oh, there he goes," Kahila suddenly said as he raised his wine glass into the air toward Joshua in a mocking fashion. "He proposes one thing in his big, mighty blog to appear like the astute gentleman of the world, but when his own daughter comes back home, not only married to a white girl, but plans on adopting children and raising them to be free spirits, he can't handle it. Why don't you just tell Tyesha and Patricia to send the kids off to boarding school when they reach puberty, then they won't have to worry about raising them at all."

"Shut the hell, boy!" Joshua yelled as he pointed his finger.

"Kahila, you need to mind your manners at this table!" Faye bellowed out. "I'll not allow that kind of talk in this dining room."

"The way we raise our children will be *our own* concern," Tyesha replied with a hot stare. "But to answer your question, daddy dearest, Patricia and I will let them grow up to be whomever they choose to be, if that be straight, gay, transgender, queer, or whatever label you choose to call it. We won't force them to be something that they don't won't to be, unlike somebody I'm currently staring at right now."

"Don't you dare talk that way to me," Joshua said with a sneer as he pointed his finger at Tyesha. "Your mother and I raised you the best way we could. You just wanted to go around and be some rebellious, promiscuous—"

"Dyke?"

"Tyesha!" Faye said with her mouth gaping wide open.

"Well, daddy dearest, this beautiful, sexy dyke is going to keep on living her life the way she chooses. She and her beautiful mate, who's sitting next to me, are going to have a long good life together. We're going to adopt as many children as we can, and we're going to raise them to be whomever they choose to be and not condemn whatever sexual preference they choose in life."

"Tyesha—"

"I'm not finished," she said as she suddenly held up her hand. "You've never accepted me for who I am, but I'm not going to make that mistake with my children. You go around proclaiming in your blog that you support the LGBT community and support us having equal rights, but you never could stand to see me being romantically involved with any of my dates growing up. And I've always been afraid to show my love with the people I've had relationships with whenever you've been around, fearing what you would say or do.

"Well, daddy dearest, that day is no more," she said audaciously. "Now that I'm a legally married woman, I'm free to openly share my love with my loving mate wherever I choose. And since you didn't get a chance to come to our marvelous wedding in Las Vegas, we're about to give you the pleasure of witnessing our true love."

Tyesha suddenly gave Patricia a long, affectionate kiss at the dining table that began to go on and on.

"Damn, Pops," Kahila said with a chuckle as he suddenly poured himself another glass of wine. "We might have to clear this dining table off of all the dishes, because it sure and hell looks like baby Sis and her new bride are ready to hop onto this table and throw down."

"Get out of this house, boy!" Joshua fumed as he glared at Kahila. "Get out right now!"

"Alright, Pops," Kahila said with a hefty chuckle. "I'm gone."

As Kahila got up to leave, Tyesha finally pulled apart from the strong embrace that she had engaged with her new wedded partner. Patricia looked totally stunned that Tyesha had embraced her with such vigorous force, but after the embrace, Tyesha merely turned and looked at her father and gave him a defiant stare.

"You don't have to throw us out, daddy dearest, because Patricia and I are leaving," Tyesha said with finality in her voice. "And we're never *ever* coming back."

As Tyesha and Patricia rose from the dining table and began to leave out of the dining room as they headed for the front door, Faye suddenly stood and looked at Joshua across the table with pleading eyes.

"Joshua, don't let them just walk—"

Joshua suddenly held up his hand to Faye. He silently shook his head as he stopped his wife in mid-sentence. Without saying a word, he rose slowly from the table and left out of the dining room. Like someone who had the weight of the world on his shoulders, he began to lumber up the winding staircase as he headed straight for his bedroom.

That night Joshua watched TV as he lay in bed. He decided to watch a movie to take his mind off his problems. Faye had drifted off to sleep beside him an hour ago, so it was just him staring through the darkness of their bedroom watching the movie. The movie was the classic comedy *Stir Crazy* starring Richard Pryor and Gene Wilder. Joshua thought it was the perfect movie to watch tonight. The way his life had been going over the last several weeks, his life was more stir crazy than anyone could imagine.

Suddenly, his cellphone on the nightstand began to ring. Joshua had been getting a few calls here and there through the night from a couple of pesky reporters, but not as many as he'd been getting over the previous nights. The main reason for the reduction in calls was because Joshua had gotten a new cellphone number, along with a new house number.

Too many overzealous reporters had constantly bombarded him with calls and had driven him up a wall, and the fact that the FBI had tapped into his cellphone and house phone made him feel violated. How the few reporters who called tonight had gotten his new cellphone number was beyond him, but Joshua knew if some pesky news reporters could somehow get his new number, then the FBI could still probably be listening in on his conversations.

Joshua picked up his cellphone and looked at the caller I.D. on the phone. The phone call had a local L.A. area code, so Joshua knew it was probably some pesky local news reporter looking to get a quick scoop.

"Hello?"

"Mr. Edwards, it's so good to hear your voice once again."

It was the raspy voice of the old man!

"Who is this?"

"Come now, Josh, good buddy," the voice said with a chuckle. "We're still playing these unnecessary games. Alright, if you must know, it's Alexander Hamilton. You know who he is?"

"Yeah, he was one of the Founding Fathers of the United States and one of the influential interpreters and promoters of the United States Constitution," Joshua said in a careful voice. "But who I believe I'm really speaking to is Bob Kramer, the head executive of the organization, Purification Of America Today."

There was suddenly a long silence over the phone.

"I see someone has been doing some homework in his spare time," the voice finally said. "Well, that's good. Now that we officially know one another, we can get straight down to business."

"I have no business with you."

"Oh, yes you do, Mr. Edwards," the voice said. "You have another interview to conduct."

"If you think I'm going to sit down and meet with any of your people again, then you're totally crazy and insane, which that's something that the entire whole world already knows as a bona fide truth anyway."

"Ah, you're referring to the incident that happened at that restaurant in St. Louis when you met with one of our faithful, loyal members who's now deceased?"

"Exactly," Joshua said in a harsh voice. "Along with thirty-seven other innocent people who didn't deserve to die, I might add."

"Well, I kind of understand your reluctance to not want to meet with us in person anymore," the man said in an easy voice, "but we don't have to publicly meet anywhere to conduct our next interview. We can do it right over the phone."

"I'm not doing anymore interviews with cold blooded murders!" Joshua suddenly said in a seething voice. "You people are nothing but the devil reincarnated. There's a place for all you rotten bastards in hell. So goodbye, *Mr. Kramer.*"

"I see you don't approve of our method of purifying this country," he said with a chuckle before Joshua could hang up. "Well, you're entitled to your opposing view. But haven't we kept our bargain of the deal when we released a child when you conducted the interview with our associate in St. Louis?"

"Some damn bargain," Joshua said in a repulsed voice. "You let one innocent child go free, but you mercilessly kill a restaurant full of people by way of some crazy suicide bomber. I don't think so, *Mr. Kramer*. Now goodbye!"

"Well, since you've decided to renege on our little deal, then there's no reason to keep these six little black bastards that we have alive," the voice said in a harsh tone. "So, goodbye to you, Mr. Edwards."

"No—"

The call suddenly went dead. Joshua held his cellphone limp in his hand when the call abruptly ended as he literally began to shake. He glanced at his wife and wondered how Faye could still sleep after the loud, voluminous conversation that he'd just had, but that wasn't the real problem.

Joshua, to his horror, suddenly realized that he may have just put those innocent little children's lives at risk. Purification Of America Today was the most evil, wretched organization that Joshua had ever witnessed or encountered. He knew without a doubt they would make good on their claim to kill those precious innocent kids without a second thought.

Literally going out of his mind with uncontrollable fear and overwhelming guilt, Joshua began pressing every button on his cellphone trying to reconnect the call, but all to no avail. His mind literally froze like an iceberg as he tried to figure out what to do, but there was no solution whatsoever.

Suddenly his cellphone once again rang. Joshua, faster than a millisecond, quickly answered his phone.

"Hello?" he said almost out of breath.

"Change your mind?" the voice of the old man said.

"Yeah . . ." Joshua said, still breathing somewhat heavily.

"Good. The topic is gun rights in America, Mr. Edwards. Come up with a list of questions and someone will contact you tomorrow morning for you to interview."

The call abruptly ended once again. Joshua, still somewhat unnerved, merely sat in his bed trying to get his wits together as the movie on the TV continued to play through the darkness of his bedroom.

Chapter 14

Joshua woke up early the next morning. He immediately began preparing questions for the interview that he was about to conduct with a member of Purification Of America Today on the topic of gun rights. He didn't know who would contact him or even what time the person would call, but Joshua wanted to be fully prepared whenever someone did call.

After jotting down a couple of questions, Joshua thought about calling the FBI to inform them he'd once again been contacted by Mr. Bob Kramer, the ring leader of Purification Of America Today, but Joshua quickly dismissed the idea. He was tired of dealing with the FBI and didn't want their intrusion. Besides, he was sure the FBI already knew he'd been contacted last night and several agents, at this very moment, were probably preparing to listen in on his conversation.

With his wife gone to one of her A Hand In Need meetings, Joshua sat alone in his bedroom watching the morning news as he waited for the contact person from Purification Of America Today to call; however, by twelve noon, no one had called and Joshua was getting restless. He wondered was anyone going to call at all when his cellphone suddenly began to ring.

Joshua, who'd been holding his cellphone in his hand virtually the entire morning, immediately looked at the caller ID. There was an unavailable number listed, and he instinctively knew it had to be the contact person finally calling.

"Hello?"

"Mr. Edwards, this is Patrick Henry calling."

Joshua didn't recognize this voice. Right off, he noticed that this caller had an aggressive tone to his voice.

"One of the Founding Fathers of our great country calling me from the year 1778," Joshua said facetiously. "How wonderful."

"A country where only the blood of the white man shall rule forevermore," he said in a confrontational tone. "A country where the mongrel race will no longer defile what is sacred in this country."

"Please, can we just get down to business?"

The caller suddenly went silent. "Absolutely," he finally said after a few seconds.

"So, we're discussing gun control in America," Joshua said as he gazed down at his notepad. "There are a few things that I wanted to—"

"No, we're discussing gun rights in America," the caller said with hostility. "You liberal fanatics have been trying to strip the people of this country of their God-given right to be armed for decades. Gun control is nothing but a synonym for the government trying to take over our lives. Well, we're not going to let that happen. Not now, not ever."

"So, I assume that Purification Of America Today opposes any gun control measures whatsoever, correct?"

"We oppose gun control one-hundred percent."

"Does that include opposing gun control measures outlawing assault rifles and other military style weapons most believe that ordinary American citizens shouldn't possess?"

"Guard with jealous attention the public liberty. Suspect everyone who approaches that jewel. Unfortunately, nothing will preserve it but downright force. Whenever you give up that force, you're ruined. The great object is that every man be armed. Everyone who is able might have a gun," he said in a lofty voice. "Do you know who said those grand words, Mr. Edwards?"

"No, I don't."

"Patrick Henry in a speech given to the Virginia Ratifying Convention on June 5th, 1778," he continued to say in a lofty voice. "It doesn't matter what style or make of a gun it may be, Mr. Edwards. Every true red blooded American has a right to be armed with whatever gun he chooses to possess."

"What about all the mass shootings that have occurred recently and throughout our nation's history when it has come to high powered weaponry in the hands of ordinary citizens, including what Purification Of America Today has murderously and criminally inflicted upon this country lately?" Joshua said harshly. "Wouldn't you site that as a reason why the Second Amendment needs to be adjusted to comply with the danger of modern mass killings?"

"The Second Amendment should *never* be touched in any way, shape, or form," he said heatedly.

"And why is that?"

"George Mason, the Father of the Bill of Rights, said to disarm the people is the most effectual way to enslave them," the caller said with an edge. "Liberals like you who have infiltrated our government have been trying to enslave this country by disarming its people. No communist revolution will ever take over this country, Mr. Edwards, because citizens who possess the right to bear arms will fight off such resistance."

"To enslave a people, you say," Joshua said with an edge. "Well, let me enlighten you and Purification Of America Today on a little history. This country long ago enslaved my forefathers and foremothers who had no arms, forced them onto ships, and brought them to this country to serve endless years of servitude. What do you say to that, *Mr. Patrick Henry?*"

"Maybe if your forefathers and foremothers were armed, maybe they wouldn't have been bonded and enslaved."

Joshua shook his head in frustration as he tried to focus on the questions he'd written on his notepad for the interview.

"The Second Amendment states that a well regulated militia being necessary to the security of a free state, the right of the people to keep and bear arms shall not be infringed," Joshua said when he glanced at his notes. "Does Purification Of America Today view themselves as some sort of militia protecting the security of a free state?"

"That's exactly who we are. We're a militia protecting the rights of true Americans and protecting the security of the state of America," the caller said heatedly. "This new liberal government is trying to rape the Constitution and strip individuals of our guns and liberties. Purification Of America Today is merely protecting what America has always stood for."

"By killing innocent people who don't fit your mode of who an American should be?"

"We're in a war, Mr. Edwards," the caller said ominously. "On the battlefield there will be many who die, but the war must be won."

"Okay, you say every American has a right to possess a gun. But what about background checks to weed out those who have criminal records or people with mental illness issues? Surely you don't propose that every single individual in America has the ultimate right to possess a gun if they're unstable."

"You mean unstable people like you, Mr. Edwards, who tried to commit suicide at a motel one night and was found the next morning with a gun lying on your chest after you'd taken a handful of pills?" the caller said sharply. "Are you talking about those type of crazy people?"

Joshua suddenly went dead silent. He was literally stunned that anyone, other than his immediate family, knew about his ordeal in that motel on that troubled, turbulent night many years ago. He definitely would never dream that a rogue terrorist organization like Purification Of America Today would know of his previous ordeal.

"Yes." Joshua swallowed hard as he finally answered. "Yes, I'm talking about people like that who may have some mental issues that they're dealing with. Surely you wouldn't propose that they should be able to attain and possess guns."

"You were redeemed and cleansed from all of your troubled demons," the caller replied in an easy voice. "Why shouldn't others who are cleansed and redeemed from their troubled demons be able to attain their God-given right to possess a gun?"

"But surely you don't—"

"The right to bear arms will not and shall not be infringed upon, Mr. Edwards!" The caller suddenly interrupted like a cold knife going through a back. "Purification Of America Today, every single one of us, will see to uphold this God-given creed if it's the last thing we do."

"But—"

"Goodbye, Mr. Edwards!" he shouted with rage. "Maybe your psychiatrist can one day help you to understand why our organization is doing what we're doing!"

The caller suddenly hung up. When the interview had ended, Joshua unconsciously let his cellphone slip from his hand as it fell to the floor. The back of his cellphone popped off as the battery scattered across the floor. Joshua knew he could reattach his phone without any problem, but he knew the sting of hearing his treacherous past thrown into his face so haphazardly, would take days to recover from.

Later that night, Joshua was in his study at his computer. He was logged into his blog, Justice For All, preparing to write his rebuttal to the gun rights in America interview that he'd conducted with the member of Purification Of America Today who'd called earlier. He titled his new blog, The Issue With Gun Rights In America. The words he wanted to say on the subject quickly began to formulate in his mind:

The Issue With Gun Rights In America

I was contacted once again by a member of Purification Of America Today to do an interview concerning gun rights in America for a child, in which this organization has kidnapped, to be released unharmed. This is my rebuttal to that interview.

Purification Of America Today states that to possess and own a gun in America is everyone's individual right as a citizen of this country, and no government authority has a right to deny that individual of that basic inherited right. They also state that no governmental restrictions should be placed on an individual's choice of the particular weapon he or she chooses to bear arms with, whether that choice of weaponry is a hand gun, basic rifle, shotgun, or a high powered assault rifle with the capacity of extreme rapid fire.

The Second Amendment states that a well regulated militia being necessary to the security of a free state, the right of the people to keep and bear arms shall not be infringed. The right of the individual to legally possess a handgun or rifle should never be infringed upon if a person does not have a criminal record and is mentally stable. However, an individual's choice to possess any assault weapon, even a semi-assault weapon which is currently legal, should never be allowed for a citizen in this country to obtain.

Evidence of mass shootings with individuals using hi-tech semi-assault weapons have been steadily on the rise in recent years. Purification Of America Today, being certified prime culprits of what a high powered weapon can do to an unsuspecting public when criminally deviant individuals get their hands on such weaponry, is a perfect example of this. The government needs to take immediate action to protect the public from such a menace. More stringent laws are needed to outlaw the surge of hi-tech weaponry steadily taking over this country.

Gun rights in America is an issue that's been simmering on the eye of the stove for decades, but now that eye is red hot and the pot is boiling over. America has had a tradition steeped in overindulgence in everything that we associate ourselves with. We want our technology smarter and more innovative, our media quicker and faster, our entertainment more glittering and scintillating, and our pleasures more extravagant and fulfilling. We have become obese from our gluttonous appetite for an endless amount food, and now we have become addicted for our appetite for more powerful, sophisticated guns.

Once again, the right to own a gun should not be infringed upon as the Second Amendment states. But our obsession to own and possess the most powerful guns the world has ever seen has now become America's new nuclear threat. The end of the cold war has terminated the previous threat of world annihilation, but America now faces the threat of weapons of mass destruction coming from within its own borders in the form of the rising hi-tech assault weaponry.

Purification Of America Today and other radicals have shown us all the danger that these weapons can have on the public in the hands of lunatics. Now it's time for new sanctions to be imposed to protect America, and those sanctions need to come in the form of more stringent gun control.

This is my rebuttal statement to the interview conducted between myself and a member of Purification Of America Today.

When Joshua finished writing his blog and sent it off so all of his millions of followers could view it, he leaned back in his chair and began to ponder. Once again, he hoped that his efforts would result in another child being released from abduction.

Joshua began to feel like he and his blog were being held hostage to satisfy the whims of a deceitful organization that didn't care one bit for human life, but if he were being held hostage, just this once, he didn't mind doing what his abductors told him to do. At least he got to state his own opinion, and most important of all, he got to play the role of hostage negotiator and help the abducted go free.

Chapter 15

The next morning, Joshua woke up and turned on his TV to the news and got a small ray of sunshine to the start off his morning; Purification Of America Today had released another kidnapped child overnight. The child, a little three-year-old girl named Olivia Lankheart, was found in an empty parking lot of a shopping mall in a suburb on the outskirts of Buffalo, NY. Once again, like the previous child found at a Philadelphia bus station a week ago, this child was in good health also. She was only terrified and wanted her mother.

Five kidnapped children taken from that Detroit daycare center still remained in the clutches of Purification Of America Today. Joshua still didn't very much like the odds of all of five remaining kids ever being freed, but as long as Purification Of America Today kept their word and continued to release a kidnapped child each time he wrote an entry in his blog after an interview, then he wasn't going to rock the boat. He was simply going to wait for the next call from the terrorist organization and continue to do his job.

Around noon, Joshua received a call from the producer of the nationally televised talk show, News Event, located in L.A. that came on across the country every week night. The producer of the show wanted Joshua to appear on tonight's show to talk about the latest developments concerning the threat that Purification Of America Today caused to the country with a panel of other national news journalists.

At first, Joshua decided to stick with his decision not to do any media interviews so as not to bring any further attention to himself, especially when those Detroit daycare kids were still being held hostage. He soon, however, reconsidered when he thought about the blog he'd written, A Treacherous Evil That Needs Resolving, that had seemed to ignite many people around the country to hit the streets and protest.

All the rioting, fighting, and chaos in many cities across the nation still went on daily, and Joshua saw an opportunity to go before the cameras and try to ask for calm and peace. He felt somewhat responsible for all the upheaval and turmoil going on, plus he was taking a mountain of criticism nightly from the press. Joshua desperately wanted to try to atone for what he'd written. He knew he couldn't hide from the crisis any longer.

Dressed in one of his nice suits, Joshua arrived at the studio an hour before airing time as he was escorted to the green waiting room so he could relax before the airing of the news show began. Two other journalists prominent in the news industry scheduled to appear on the show tonight as co-panelists, were already in the green room. Joshua immediately began to make small talk with the journalists as they passed the time.

When another co-panelist scheduled to appear on the show suddenly entered the green room, Joshua's jaw immediately dropped in disbelief. Conrad, all six-foot-five three hundred pounds of him, was dressed in a nice conservative suit. He had a seat next to Joshua like a big, important man who'd arrived for a CEO meeting. Joshua glanced at his brother when Conrad picked up a magazine from a rack next to him as he began to flip through the pages. Joshua was so stupefied at seeing his brother, he almost couldn't speak.

"What in the world are you doing here?" Joshua asked in a flabbergasted voice.

Conrad continued to slowly flip through the pages of the magazine. "You think you're the only big shot in the family who has some pull around here and can speak on the issues at hand?" he said in a lofty, arrogant voice as he continued to flip through the pages of the magazine. "You're not the only one whose name happens to be Edwards."

Joshua could only close his eyes and sigh to himself. He knew without a doubt that tonight was going to be one argumentative, contentious affair.

The national telecast of the talk show, News Event, got underway as the host, Holly Mitchell, asked some tough questions to her panel of four. Her panel consisted of John Parkington, an award winning journalist for a New York magazine; Bill Sturtevant, a political reporter from Washington; Conrad Edwards, host of the local Los Angeles conservative radio talk show, Talk Back Today; and, of course, Joshua Edwards, writer of the blog, Justice For All, and author of several bestselling books.

The discussion among the panel of four was engaging on all sides of the issues. The host delved into the areas concerning Joshua's blog, the interview he conducted at the soul food restaurant in St. Louis that ended tragically, what took place presently in the country with all the riots and fighting in the streets, and what Purification Of America Today was doing.

"Joshua Edwards," the host said when she turned to him, "when you wrote that entry into your blog that you titled, A Treacherous Evil That Needs Resolving, what did you hope to accomplish?"

"On that particular evening that I wrote that entry into my blog, I'd just been contacted by a member of Purification Of America Today earlier that day. Those seven little African American children from that daycare center in Detroit had just been kidnapped, and the leader of

Purification Of America Today demanded that I write a rebuttal in my blog to a number of positions that they passionately stood for as a condition for the kidnapped children they were holding to be set free," Joshua said to the host. "I was highly upset that these scoundrels had kidnapped these innocent little children and were, in fact, holding me somewhat responsible for their well-being. They were blackmailing me to get involved in their twisted, evil plans, and I'd had enough.

"I wrote from a place of sheer anger and fury, and I somewhat let my emotions get the best of me," Joshua said as he continued. "I never dreamed that my mere words would cause such rage in people across the country to literally take to the streets and provoke violence upon one another and upon our towns and cities in the fashion that has taken place."

"So what you're saying is that you're retracting from your position that you stated in your blog entry, A Treacherous Evil That Needs Resolving?"

"Yes, Holly, I am," he said in a sincere voice. "We all make mistakes when we're under duress, and I sincerely want to ask America for calm and peace during this terrible ordeal that our country is going through. Violence doesn't achieve a true resolution. It only precipitates more anarchy and chaos."

"Mr. Parkington, do you believe that the violence and chaos that have ensued in the streets of America would've happened anyway if Joshua Edwards hadn't stirred the pot with his inflammatory blog?"

"That's hard to say," the journalist said as he mused over the question. "We've had many radical, racist groups and anti-government organizations to have come out of the wood works and hit the streets in numbers since Purification Of America Today started all of these terrorist attacks. Marchers and protestors, who've been in the streets protesting what Purification Of America Today has been doing lately, have come in direct contact with a lot of these racist hate groups. Quite naturally, altercations and provocations between the two are going to happen. It's just a cause and a reaction type of thing."

"Do you believe marshal law should be instituted around America to prevent further bloodshed and anarchy from happening in the streets?"

"Yes, I do. We're in a state of emergency, and until this crisis can be peacefully settled, certain segments of America's streets need to be put in a lockdown mode."

"Mr. Sturtevant, you've been a political reporter and a journalist in Washington for a number of years. What are the political ramifications you believe will come out of this as a result of what's been happening?"

"The threat of home grown terrorism from radical hate groups and anti-government organizations has been on the rise over the last decade," the journalist said with a pensive face. "A lot of these groups and organizations have been operating in the dark shadows of society for a number of years. Now that Purification Of America Today has come out from the dark shadows into the open and has caused the sheer amount of terror that it has brought upon America, other groups are more likely to become copycat terrorist groups in the future.

"Congress will more likely enact new laws and measures to totally eliminate these groups and organizations from even forming," he said as he continued. "A lot of people's First Amendment rights could very well be imposed on, and I'm sure these extremist groups will scream and shout that their right to exercise their beliefs are being trampled on, but in light of what's been taking place, you very well could see a radical change and shift in laws to protect America against the rise of homegrown terrorism."

"Would this shift affect the Republican base more or the Democrat base?"

"I believe it will affect both."

"Mr. Edwards, you're a host of a conservative radio talk show in the

Los Angeles area," the host said when she turned to Conrad. "What do your callers say that has led to the rise of so many radical hate groups and extreme anti-government organizations in this country?"

"The liberal agenda in this country has been manipulating and twisting the moral values in this country so much in recent years, until America has almost become an entirely new and different nation altogether," Conrad said with simmering passion. "This movement away from traditional values that this country once stood for has birthed a movement of resentment and hatred in some segments of society. It has become the linchpin that's set off the bomb that's exploded in America."

"So your callers site a breakdown of traditional core values as the reason why some of these radical hate groups have popped up over the years?"

"Absolutely."

"Concerning all the rioting and fighting that we've seen lately in the streets, do you see this as somewhat of a new sort of civil war between the extreme left and the extreme right that's going on in America? Do you believe that the beliefs and principles of the two opposing forces that have been on a collision course for years, have finally clashed at this point and time to settle which side will have the most influence on the future of American culture and politics?"

"Instead of a civil war, I see this more as Armageddon."

"Armageddon?"

"That's right."

"That's pretty extreme, Mr. Edwards. Why Armageddon?"

"Because the liberal movement, if they win, will completely destroy this country and take it down to utter ruins," Conrad said in an unwavering voice. "When you have a liberal proponent who has a huge voice in his arena who calls for his soldiers to sharpen their swords and hit the streets, that's calling for an annihilation of America's integrity and an end to the morals and values that this country cherishes and holds sacred. It's a call to annihilate our sacred freedom."

"You're referring to your brother's blog, Justice For All?"

"Absolutely," Conrad said without hesitation. "He's virtually set himself up as a demigod, declaring war on American society. He's no different than a ruthless dictator who has twisted the minds of his followers to commit acts of unnecessary violence to further his aims and goals."

"Now hold on," Joshua said, suddenly chiming in. "I've already granted that I spoke on pure emotion that evening because of my feelings toward those children being kidnapped, but I've never called for an annihilation of America's morals and values. That's just a bunch of hogwash."

"You're constantly propagating vain and immoral rhetoric to advance your liberal agenda," Conrad said in a chastising voice. "The moral fiber of this country is going down fast because of unrestrained liberals like you who have no mouthpiece to stop your unscrupulous notions and rantings."

"I beg your pardon," Joshua said heatedly. "You're the one who can't seem to accept anyone else's views other than your own. The far right wing conservatives are the people who are giving these extreme hate groups the ammunition to commit such dastardly deeds on American society."

"Don't perpetrate like you're innocent in polluting the minds of the people who read your blog."

"Gentlemen—"

"I'm not perpetrating anything," Joshua said full of wrath. "I only speak the unvarnished truth to the people out there who want to listen to the issues at hand. I don't dictate anything to anyone. The people make up their own minds on the issues that affect us."

"Gentlemen—"

"You're a loose cannon who needs to be checked. We have a total mess in the streets of America because you've inflamed a bunch of thugs and hoodlums to commit violence."

"Gentlemen—"

"Are you calling hard working, honest Americans who have a right to protest against terror and injustice hooligans and thugs?"

"No, but I'm calling you a tyrannical rebel rouser who creates divisive situations so thugs and hoodlums can have a reason to go out in the streets to stir up violence and chaos."

"How dare you!"

"Gentlemen, please," the host finally said as she raised her voice. "Let's have a civil dialogue here."

When the host was finally able to silence her two panelists of their acrimonious debate, the news show suddenly went to a commercial break. When the show resumed after the commercial break however, the intense bickering between the two Edward brothers only continued.

Chapter 16

Joshua arrived at his psychiatrist's office early the next morning for his regular first of the month visit. Dr. Harold Mitchell once again greeted Joshua like a dear old friend when Joshua entered the office. The two looked like they'd had plenty of deep, private conversations over the years by the way they warmly shook hands.

"Josh, so good to see you," he said, patting his friend on the shoulder. "I saw you and your brother last night on News Event. I'm sure you two have given the show plenty of good overnight ratings by the way you two were clawing at each other," he said with a light-hearted chuckle.

"They set me up, Doc," Joshua said as he shook his head. "They asked me to come on the show yesterday to talk about what's been going on around the country, but I had no idea Conrad was going to be one of the panel members. If I'd known he was going to be on the show, I would've definitely turned down the offer."

"And ruin all the fireworks that exploded between you two," Dr. Mitchell said with an amusing smile. "The entire country would've missed the best reality show on TV."

"It seemed to me more like a circus freak show or some zoo exhibit than an invite to do a talk on the state of affairs around the country."

"I can certainly imagine it did."

When Joshua had a seat in the chair in front of Dr. Mitchell's glass desk, the psychiatrist had a seat behind his desk and began his conversation.

"Speaking of the state of the country, let's talk about that blog you wrote, A Treacherous Evil That Needs Resolving."

"Is this another interview, Doc?"

"Not exactly." Dr. Mitchell chuckled. "I just wanted to get a sense on how you felt after you wrote that particular blog when you noticed all the rioting, fighting, and clashes started happening in the streets. Quite frankly, how did it affect your psyche?"

"I was angry when I wrote that particular piece in my blog, Doc. It made me so upset that Purification Of America Today would link me into their web of evil and deceit and hold me responsible for the well-being of those kidnapped kids. I wrote from a place of anger that I shouldn't have."

"But how did it affect your psyche?"

"You mean did it make me want to grab a gun and a bottle of pills and go check into a motel for the night?" Joshua said sarcastically. "Are you about ready to call the mental ward and make reservations for me, Doc?"

"You know what I mean, Josh," Dr. Mitchell said with a chuckle.

"I don't know," Joshua said as he suddenly gazed up at the office ceiling, pondering deeply. "I said what I said that day. For as how it affected me, I can live with it."

"Okay, well, let me ask you a more poignant question," Dr. Mitchell said in a more subdued voice. "How did it make you feel that day when you ran out of that restaurant when that suicide bomber blew up the place and you knew all of those people had just been killed?"

"It made me feel fortunate, utterly sick to my stomach, and guilty."

"Guilty as of how?"

"That I didn't see what was coming when I was interviewing that man," Joshua said as he continued to stare at the ceiling. "Somehow it made me feel that I was a co-contributor to all of those people being murdered."

"By not knowing that man had a pack of explosives strapped to his body underneath his sweater?"

"Yes."

"Joshua, you must not feel responsible for the deaths of those people in that restaurant," Dr. Mitchell said in a calm voice. "You were trying to help get those kidnapped children released. Your intentions were noble and heroic. You were fighting the good fight. You weren't some mercenary paid to fight some unjust war."

"Yeah, but what good is it to get one or two kidnapped children released from their abductors, Doc, when a restaurant full of people lose their lives as a result of your efforts?" Joshua said when he finally took his gaze from the ceiling and gave his psychiatrist a scathing look. "I actually do feel like a mercenary soldier who's caused considerable collateral damage to a lot of innocent lives."

"Josh, do you remember a number of years ago when we had a conversation about how those 9/11 firemen went into one of those burning towers and found a somewhat older woman who had trouble making it down those flight of stairs? The building was beginning to creak and crumble only minutes before it collapsed. Do you remember that discussion?"

"Yeah, I remember."

"Do you remember how those brave firefighters stayed with that woman until the very end, even when the tower collapsed, but they still somehow managed to survive in that massive rumble and get out of there with that woman alive and well?"

"Yeah, I remember that."

"Those firemen didn't stay with that woman because it was their job. They stayed with her because they cared. And that's what you are, Josh, a fireman."

"A fireman?"

"Yes," Dr. Mitchell said as he stared at Joshua with sympathy. "You're a fireman who cares about those children's well-being. You've been repeatedly going into a burning building saving one little life after another from utter destruction. You're a fireman who cares, Josh, and you must always remember that. Don't look at it as you've caused collateral damage, because that's simply not so. You've been a fireman who's cared about saving and preserving life, and you've done just that."

Joshua and Dr. Mitchell talked further about the tension and stress that Joshua had been under dealing with Purification Of America Today. The entire time, the psychiatrist constantly gave positive reinforcement to his good friend and longtime patient.

About an hour and a half later, Joshua and Dr. Mitchell had covered all the infinite details and intricacies of Purification Of America Today probably better than the FBI. They were all talked out on the subject at hand.

"Well, Josh, I don't believe we've had this long of a session in quite a while," Dr. Mitchell said as he gazed down at his appointment book on his desk. "I believe I've made my eleven o'clock appointment wait over for nearly thirty minutes."

"You're telling me to get the hell out, Doc?"

"Josh, you know I'd clean my entire appointment book for you," Dr. Mitchell said with sincerity. "There's never been any time limit with us."

"Yeah, but the damn meter has always been running," Joshua said in jest. "I believe I've paid for half of this beautiful luxurious twelfth floor suite you have up here, Doc."

"Well, maybe just a little," Dr. Mitchell said with a smile and a wink. "Tell me, Josh, how did that Sunday dinner go with your daughter, Tyesha, and her newly wedded mate? Did everything go alright?"

Joshua suddenly let out a long, deep sigh. For the longest, he just sat in his chair staring at Dr. Mitchell. From his dismal expression, it looked like he'd just taken a powerful sock straight to the gut.

"You know, Doc, I think I'd rather run out of a restaurant again with only seconds until the place blew up than to have another Sunday dinner with Tyesha and her wedded mate," he said in agony. "In fact, if we did ever have another Sunday dinner, I think I'd wear some explosives tied around me so I can blow my own self up."

"It went that bad, huh?"

Joshua slowly nodded. "That bad, Doc."

"Well, remember, Josh, if you want to ever save the relationship you have with your daughter, you're going to have to pull her, along with her new mate, up from that steep cliff that they're hanging from," he said in a serious tone. "They're both linked together. You're just going to have to be strong, Josh. You're going to have to ignore the resentment you may have concerning that situation if you want to reconcile the relationship that you have with your daughter."

"I hear you, Doc," Joshua said with a deep sigh. "But it ain't easy."

Joshua and Faye were having dinner in a fancy, upscale restaurant in Beverly Hills. The restaurant was packed with well-dressed professional people eating and having light conversation while soft music played overhead. Joshua and Faye tried to enjoy their time together away from the house. They hadn't been out for a nice dinner in quite a while, and as they ate and conversed with one another at their table, they tried their best not to once mention nor even think about Purification Of America Today.

Not thinking about that wretched, miserable nemesis that had encroached into their lives over the last several weeks, however, was a tall order. It was especially hard when most of the people in the restaurant constantly whispered and stared at their table.

"Well, I guess everyone in this place is having a good conversation at their table discussing the world's most notorious celebrity who happens to be eating in this fancy restaurant," Joshua said as he slowly scanned all the people whispering and staring at their table. "I can imagine all the vile things they're probably saying."

"Try to ignore them," Faye said as she dug her fork into her Caesar Salad. "We're here to enjoy a nice dinner, remember?"

"How can I ignore them? Look at them," Joshua said, shaking his head in frustration. "They're probably saying, 'Look, there's that idiot who started all the riots and fights that are going on in the streets all over the country,' or they're saying, 'He should be ashamed of himself for letting Purification Of America Today use him to further their objectives. He ain't doing nothing but aiding their cause.' Yeah, I know what they're sitting around saying, Faye."

"Joshua, will you stop it," Faye said in a riled voice as she tried to keep her voice down at the table. "I didn't come here to talk about nothing that's even remotely connected with that damn Purification Of America Today. Now I came here to have a pleasant, peaceful dinner."

"But, Faye—"

"No!" she said, suddenly giving him a stern eye across the table. "Now I've had enough."

"Alright, I'm sorry," he said with a sigh as he continued eating his meal. "Okay, so what do you want to talk about then?"

"How about my upcoming trip to New York for the A Hand In Need convention that I'm going to be gone for four days to?" Faye said when she eyed her husband. "Why don't we talk about that?"

"Oh, wow." Joshua suddenly glanced across the table completely embarrassed. "I've totally forgotten about that."

"You're not the only one who has an agenda in this life," Faye said in an irritated voice. "Other people have things that are important in their lives, too."

"You're right. I'm sorry, Faye," he said apologetically. "When do you suppose to leave?"

"Our national convention is coming up in two weeks. I'm leaving on the—"

Joshua's attention was suddenly diverted toward the front entrance of the restaurant. His eyes immediately began to narrow as he glared at what he saw. "I'll be damn."

"What is it?"

"Look."

Conrad and his wife, Lacy, had suddenly entered the posh Beverly Hills restaurant. The maître d' checked their reservations and began to escort them to their table. As the maître d' led the way, Joshua could tell that Conrad and Lacy were getting ready to head straight pass their table.

"Please don't start anything." Faye implored as she quickly gazed across the table at Joshua with pleading eyes. "We came here for a nice dinner and nothing else."

"That pompous sonofabitch."

"Joshua, please."

Soon as the maître d' approached Joshua and Faye's table with his guests, Conrad and Lacy suddenly stopped. They were well dressed just like everyone else in the packed restaurant. Conrad and Lacy certainly did look like two prosperous pillars of society.

"Well, this is quite a surprise," Conrad said as he stared down at Joshua and Faye's dinner table.

"A very unpleasant one," Joshua said with venom in his voice when he looked up at his brother.

"Hi, Faye," Lacy said in a somewhat nervous voice. "I didn't know you two would be here."

"Yeah, we decided to get out of the house tonight," Faye said in a courteous voice as she quickly smiled. "Imagine running into you two here."

"It's a small world."

"You can say that again," Joshua said with an attitude. He tried to ignore his brother and his wife standing at their table as he continued eating.

"They say the lobster is great here," Conrad said with a smile. "What do you suggest, little bro?"

"Look, Conrad, you're holding up traffic," Joshua said as he glanced at the maître d' who waited patiently for Conrad and Lacy to finish their conversation so he could escort the two of them to their table. "I believe your table is ready."

"You know last night, I really took you to school," Conrad said in a smug voice, ignoring the maître d' who stood patiently beside him and his wife. "You should've heard all the callers who called into my radio show today. They said I waxed you something good."

"You mean all fifty callers that your little radio show has," Joshua said in a needling voice.

"What?"

"Honey, let's just go to our table." Faye insisted as she pulled on Conrad's arm.

"That's a good idea. You should listen to your wife," Joshua said in a flippant voice as he continued eating. "You do one national talk show and now you think you're the conservative Rush Limbaugh."

"And what the hell does that supposed to mean?"

"It means you don't have the balls to play in my league, big bro," Joshua said as he finally looked back up at Conrad. "So why don't you run on back to the junior league where you belong."

"And I guess you think you're some hot ass journalist just because you got a few million followers who follow your damn blog?"

"It's a few million more than you have."

"Well, anyone who causes major riots and fights in streets all over America is not a journalist in my book," Conrad said as he glared down at Joshua. "In my book, he's nothing but a two bit hack who needs to be locked up in prison for inciting and instigating riots and mayhem."

"Hey, you watch what you say to me," Joshua said in a hostile voice as he suddenly pointed his finger at Conrad, "because you don't know a damn thing of what you're talking about."

"Yeah, you're right. Let me correct myself," Conrad said in an antagonistic voice. "You're nothing but a two bit whore for that Purification Of America Today to do as they say. They've been screwing your ass so hard lately, you won't have to go to prison to be somebody's lover boy."

Joshua suddenly rose from the table and began to charge at his brother swinging both fists. A hellish altercation quickly ensued as the customers, eating their expensive meals, watched in horror as a street brawl literally began to take place inside the fancy, packed restaurant.

Chapter 17

Joshua and his brother were handcuffed, arrested, and taken to jail. The raucous episode at one of Beverly Hills' finest restaurants quickly made waves through the media circle. The buzz going around was not only the author of the blog Justice For All was good at inciting mayhem and unrest in American streets, but he was also good at creating turmoil inside a fancy, upscale restaurant.

The next morning when Faye was finally able to bail her husband out of jail and they returned home, Joshua went straight to his bedroom and went to bed. Quickly realizing that spending all night inside a jail cell with some of L.A.'s most harden criminals had made him too restless and wired up to sleep, he hastily rose from bed as he grabbed his keys and left the house. He hopped into his Jaguar, cranked the motor, and left out of the driveway as he headed for Sam's Rib Shack.

When Joshua had driven across town and stopped at a red light at an intersection, he was suddenly rammed from behind. Joshua looked into his rear view mirror and saw that a white van had run into the back of him. He sighed and immediately began cursing up a storm, knowing that some idiot driver was probably too busy talking on his cellphone and hadn't watched where he was going.

Angry that his night had been spent sitting in a jail cell and now his morning was starting off miserably, Joshua got out from behind the wheel of his Jaguar to check on the damage to his car. Soon as he approached the rear of his Jaguar, three men suddenly jumped out of the rear of the white van. Two of the men, who were of huge size, quickly seized him as the other man jumped into his car.

"Hey, what the hell is this?" Joshua yelled in rage when the men clamped and restrained his arms behind his back. "Let go of me!"

The men ignored Joshua's complaints as they forced him into the back of the white van and closed the door. Within seconds, the van, along with Joshua's Jaguar, sped away from the intersection.

Faye began to worry that something had happened to Joshua. For the past eight hours, she'd been trying to contact her husband on his cellphone, but each time she'd phone him, his voice message would pick up.

Four hours ago, she'd called Sam's Rib Shack to see if he'd been there, but Big Sam said he hadn't been by all day. Faye knew that Joshua liked to roam about and have his freedom from time to time, but he would never resort to not call to inform her of where he was. He always stayed connected to her, and she always stayed connected with him. For as him seeing another woman, she knew that possibility was remote. Joshua had long ago stopped chasing the skirts of other women and was now a family man to the letter. No, something was wrong. Faye could feel it inside of her that something wasn't right.

When nightfall began to set in, Faye finally contacted the police to inform them of her husband's situation. Normally the police said they would rather prefer to wait a full twenty-four hours before taking any action on a missing person, but considering the unusual situation that Joshua had been under over the last several weeks, they weren't taking any chances.

Faye began pacing back and forth in her kitchen as she waited for the police to arrive to further question her. She couldn't sit down for one second because her nerves had gotten her all twisted and nervous. Her nerves literally felt like coils of rope tightening around her tighter and tighter as she continued to pace.

Soon as the doorbell rang, Faye moved quickly out of the kitchen and headed through the foyer for the front door. When she opened the door, she found a policeman and three FBI agents standing on her porch.

"Mrs. Edwards, I'm Agent Dale Gatewood from the Federal Bureau of Investigation," he said as he showed her his badge. "We'd like to ask you a few questions concerning your husband."

"Yes, please, come in."

Faye let the policeman and the three FBI agents into the parlor. The head FBI agent immediately began interrogating.

"Mrs. Edwards, when was the last time you spoke to your husband?"

"Early this morning," Faye said in a worried voice. "I'd just bailed him out of jail and we had returned home. He tried to sleep for a while, but couldn't, so he decided to go to Sam's Rib Shack in Crenshaw to hang out for a while."

"Did he ever make it to that destination?"

"I called the owner, but he said Joshua had never been there today."

"Do you think your husband could be off seeing someone else?"

"You mean another woman?"

"Yes."

"No." Faye quickly shook her head. "Something else has happened."

"Has anyone called demanding money?"

"You think he's been kidnapped?" Faye asked as she stared at the agent frightfully.

"It's a possibility."

"Well, what's the FBI going to do about this?" she said in a trembling voice. "You've got to get my husband back."

"Right now, Mrs. Edwards, we don't know for sure if your husband has been kidnapped," the agent said. "But we'll begin procedures to try to locate him. Over the last couple of weeks, your husband has been quite visible in the news. He's become quite a target, Mrs. Edwards. Anyone might just try to nab him for the sheer publicity or hold him hostage to try to seek a monetary deal."

"This is not beginning to sound good," Faye suddenly said. She rubbed her temples as her stomach began to feel like rotten poison smoldered inside it. "It's not sounding good not one bit."

"Mrs. Edwards, police officer Bill Myers here will be stationed outside in his police car in front of your house for your protection through the night." He pointed to the policeman standing next to the FBI agents. "It's imperative that you not be alone at this juncture when your husband could be in grave danger. You could quite well be a target yourself."

Faye merely nodded as she held her stomach.

"Well, we'll be on our way for now, ma'am," the agent said. He and his fellow agents began to head out of the parlor. "We'll be in touch."

When the FBI agents and the police officer left out of the house, Faye closed the front door and quickly hurried to the bathroom. The rotten, vile feeling in her stomach felt like it was about to come up at any second.

Chapter 18

By nightfall, Joshua's horrendous ordeal still continued. He'd been blindfolded and gagged since forced inside the white van when it sped away from that intersection. His abductors had driven a hundred miles from Los Angeles where they arrived at a private airstrip. From there the abductors, along with their blindfolded hostage, boarded a private jet plane and took off.

Four hours later when they finally landed, the abductors took their kidnapped hostage by van to a remote destination deep in the woods. When they arrived at their intended location, they took their kidnapped hostage inside a secluded complex, placed him in a room, and tied him to a chair. Since then, Joshua sat alone in this room tied to a chair nervous, scared, and hungry.

After being blindfolded for nearly the entire day and tied to a chair for nearly six hours, someone suddenly yanked off Joshua's blindfold. Joshua strained to focus his eyesight as the bright light in the room blinded him. When his blurry eyesight finally began to focus more clearly, Joshua saw twelve figures sitting at a long table. Each member was donned in black jumpsuits wearing an orange mask with a picture of a white skeleton and crossbones plastered on the forehead of the mask.

Joshua quickly scanned the room and noticed candles were lit everywhere. The room had a cryptic, mysterious vibe to it as all sorts of racist propaganda was scrawled on the walls in various colors. It seemed like a kid had gotten a box of crayons and had gone wild drawing designs on the walls. On the ceiling was a statement in bold words that said: THE RED, WHITE, AND BLUE WILL NEVER BE SMEARED OR STAINED AGAIN.

Suddenly the figure sitting in the middle of the table among the masked men pulled off his mask and revealed his face. He was an older Caucasian man who looked to be in his mid-eighties. He had a pleasant smile as he looked at Joshua, who was still tied to the chair. His disposition seemed to be one of a gentle, old man who had no concerns or worries in the world.

"Well, hello, Mr. Edwards," the gentle, old man said in a raspy voice.

Joshua immediately recognized the voice, but still he had to ask. "Who are you?"

"I'm Bob Kramer," he said with a smile, "head executive of Purification Of America Today."

Joshua once again slowly scanned the table of all the masked figures donned in black jumpsuits and orange masks. The image of the white skeletons and crossbones stapled to the forehead of each mask seemed so strange and puzzling.

"Why am I here?" Joshua asked in a troubled voice. "Why have you kidnapped me and brought me to this place?"

"Because, Mr. Edwards, you're about to become a certified member of our great organization, Purification Of America Today."

"I'm what?"

"Gentlemen," the old man said with a smile, "please begin."

Three massive brutes suddenly appeared from behind Joshua and quickly untied the rope from around him. As two of the massive brutes firmly held him down steady in the chair, one of the massive brutes took a red hot branding iron and branded the letters P.O.A.T. on his right forearm. Joshua let out a vicious scream of agony from the pulsating hot burn to his forearm as he was quickly retied to the chair when they finished.

Still cringing in agony, Joshua looked at the smiling old man sitting at the table with pain beaming from his eyes.

"What the hell is this all about?" he said, breathing heavily. "You people are crazy!"

"No we're not, Mr. Edwards," the old man said with a chuckle. "You see, now that you're about to become a full member of our organization, you'll be supporting our cause and our great mission. We need someone of your talent and skill to tell the public the views of how Purification Of America Today feels about certain issues in a powerful, persuasive way. Now that you have millions and millions of people who constantly follow your blog on a weekly basis, you'll be able to tell our point of view in a powerful way that only you could tell in such elegant words. It's the least you can do, since we helped you attain such a large, prosperous following."

"No way will I ever do that," Joshua said with a sneer. "Never!"

"Oh, you will, Mr. Edwards. You will," the old man said with a chuckle. "Now, you must meet your other brothers of Purification Of America Today who are sitting here at this table. As you probably already know, Purification Of America Today has several other chapters in other states around the country, but the brothers you're about to meet here are our highest ranking members. They follow my orders, and in turn, they give out my corresponding orders to the chapters they represent in other states," he said in a business-like voice. "Now, it's time to meet your new brothers. Gentlemen, let's get started."

The orange mask from the figure sitting at the far right was suddenly removed. Each member followed suit while they went down the line of the long table as each member introduced himself.

"I'm Joe Lillard, P.O.A.T. member since 2008."

"Kyle Peyton, P.O.A.T. member since 2007."

"Jim Ellington, P.O.A.T. member since 2006."

"Frank Barnes, P.O.A.T. member since 2005."

"Eddie Lawrence, P.O.A.T. member since 2009."

"Don Ewing, P.O.A.T. member since 2007."

"Victor Zimmerman, P.O.A.T. member since 2004."

"Denny Smith, P.O.A.T. member since 2006."

"Buford Long, P.O.A.T. member since 2007."

"Peter Cook, P.O.A.T. member since 2008."

"Chester Washington, P.O.A.T. member since 2011."

"Mr. Z, P.O.A.T. member since 2007."

When Joshua suddenly saw the last member pull off his orange mask and reveal the huge tattoo on his forehead that said KILL NIGGERS, he couldn't believe his eyes. It was actually Mr. Z, the inmate he'd just visited a week ago at the Los Angeles jail.

Of all the white faces staring at him in a foreboding, ominous way from the long table in front of him, Joshua couldn't seem to take his eyes away from the one named Mr. Z. That wild, mangy hair streaking all the way down his back was certainly an eyesight, but those smoldering, penetrating eyes he could never forget. Even when Mr. Z sat behind that glass partition at the L.A. jail that day, Joshua could still feel those smoldering eyes burning straight through that thick glass. As they stared at one another at the present moment, those smoldering, penetrating eyes still felt like blazing fire staring straight in his direction.

"Brothers of Purification Of America Today," the old man said, "if you accept Joshua Edwards as a member of our organization, say I."

"I!" rang out from all twelve men sitting at the table.

"Congratulations, Mr. Edwards. You're now an official member of our great organization," the old man said proudly. "Oh, and there's one other reason why we chose you to join our wonderful organization. We needed to integrate our membership. That's what our government says that corporations must do these days in this country. They say organizations like ours must confirm to affirmative action. And you can bet your bottom dollar, Mr. Edwards, we're certainly going to make the most of it."

A ruckus, raunchy laugh suddenly exploded around the long table as Joshua looked on in horror.

Joshua was locked in a small room no bigger than a utility closet that contained a heavy steel door. He lay on a hard, uncomfortable cot as he stared through the darkness of the room. Even though his stomach growled in desperate need of something to eat, he was at least thankful that he wasn't tied down any longer. Just being able to move his arms around freely after being roped up like a calf for nearly the entire day felt liberating. His arms may have still been somewhat sore, but at least they were free.

As Joshua lay there on his cot staring at the darkness, he couldn't help but think about Faye. He knew she had to be worried to death. They had always stayed in contact with one another no matter where the other went. It was highly unusual for either of them not to call the other after four or five hours had passed. After five hours had passed and neither person hadn't called the other to just check on their mate's day, that was like an eternity.

It wasn't always like that, but over the years their marriage had evolved into such a strong, loving connection. At the moment, however, there was no way he could get in contact with Faye and tell her, under the circumstances, that he wasn't alright. Hopefully the authorities were making an effort to try to find him. They had to know by now that Purification Of America Today had probably taken him and was holding him hostage.

Suddenly, as he lay on his cot staring in the darkness of his cramped room, Joshua began to hear a certain sound coming through his wall. At first the sound was indecipherable, then before he knew it, the sound became more pronounced the louder it grew. Within a few seconds, Joshua could clearly make out what the sound was, and it was clearly the reverberation of little children wailing and crying.

Joshua quickly realized that it had to be those kidnapped children from that Detroit daycare center in the very room next to him. Their constant crying and calls for their mothers began to hurt Joshua's heart more than a massive heart attack. He began to realize that his own anxiety and discomfort were nothing in comparison to what those little precious souls were probably going through. They had been away from their mothers for weeks now, and all the wretched misery and grief constantly being put on their young minds nightly had to be just downright unbearable.

As Joshua continued to listen to the painful cries of the children in the room next to him, a small slot on the heavy steel door of his room slid open. A voice on the other side of the door suddenly whispered his name. Joshua, through the darkness, began to squint at the heavy steel door to try to see who it was.

"Yeah, who is it?"

"It's Zack," the voice whispered on the other side of the door.

"Who?"

"Mr. Z."

Joshua slowly rose from the cot as he went to the heavy steel door. He peered through the small slit of the door and saw the wild, mangy haired inmate he'd visited at the L.A. jail on the other side of the door. Even through the darkness, he could still see the KILL NIGGERS tattoo on his forehead.

"I thought you were supposed to be in jail," Joshua said in an alarmed voice. "What are you doing here?"

"I got out a few days ago," he whispered. "And keep your damn voice down."

"So, did you help the good brothers of your organization in the planning of kidnapping me?" Joshua whispered angrily through the slot.

"I didn't know anything about you being brought here," he whispered back. "I was just as shocked to see you here as you were to see me."

"That's real comforting to know," Joshua whispered back sarcastically. "So, Mr. Z—"

"Just call me Zack."

"Alright, *Mr. Zack*," Joshua whispered loudly. "Where are we? Are we in Virginia at that compound that Purification Of America Today has that you were telling me about back at the jail?"

"No, we're in Ohio."

"Ohio?"

"Yeah, we're at a compound about fifty miles south of Cleveland."

"You didn't say anything about Purification Of America Today having a compound in Ohio."

"Hey, I've been in jail for nearly a year," he whispered back. "We didn't have a compound here in Ohio back then. Things change while you're in jail, you know."

"I guess that makes sense."

"Listen," Mr. Z whispered. "I'm going to help you get out of here."

"What about those kidnapped kids in the room next to me?"

"I don't know if I can do anything about them."

"You've got to help me and those kids get out of here," Joshua whispered. "The sooner the better."

"That's going to be nearly impossible," Mr. Z whispered back. "This place is pretty well guarded. I believe I can sneak you out of here, but trying to sneak those kids out too is going to be too tall of a task. That's just not going to—"

"Listen to me!" Joshua whispered loudly. "I'm not leaving here without those kids. Now, you're just going to have to find a way. You hear me?"

Mr. Z was suddenly silent. As the silence went on, Joshua waited impatiently for a reply.

"Alright," he finally whispered back. "You're going to have to be patient. I'll try to think of something."

"We don't have a lot of time to be patient!"

"You don't have a damn choice."

The small slot to the door suddenly closed shut. When his unexpected visitor had abruptly departed, Joshua stumbled back through the darkness as he reclined once again on the hard, uncomfortable cot. Still too restless and stressed out for any sleep, Joshua just stared at the room's ceiling. Unable to do anything else, he slowly began to count the minutes until he and those defenseless innocent kids in the room next to him could be free.

Chapter 19

The next morning, Joshua was allowed to shower and given a change of clothes. He was then fed a big, hearty breakfast that would put a five star hotel to shame. Hotel Purification Of America Today may give their guests crummy, tight accommodations, but they served the best breakfast in all of America.

After he was fed, Joshua was led to the other side of the compound to a particular office by two huge bodyguards. When Joshua entered the office, he saw Bob Kramer, the eighty-six-year-old head executive of Purification Of America Today, sitting behind a desk.

Joshua took the liberty to quickly glance around the office. The office had all sorts of famous art paintings along the walls of various historical achievements and well-known events throughout American history. To take a glance at this wall in this particular office was like taking a walk down the hall of a Smithsonian museum. Glorious battles, famous presidential inaugurations, the first landing on the moon, and other momentous American events and occasions bristled all along the walls of the office like the Fourth of July.

"Mr. Edwards," the old gentleman behind the desk said with a smile. "So glad to see you on this gorgeous early morning. Please, have a seat."

Joshua had a seat in the chair located near the desk as the two huge bodyguards fell back and took up a position near the office door.

"Well, Mr. Edwards, you look well rested," the old gentleman said with a generous smile. "How did you sleep?"

"I slept all of about thirty minutes on a hard cot, and now I have a crook in my back."

"So sorry to hear that. I hope the breakfast made up for the bad sleeping arrangement."

"It was superb," Joshua said in a flat voice.

"That's wonderful," the old gentleman said in a cheery voice. "We try to treat our new members to the best amenities available. Would you care for any coffee, juice, or tea?"

"Not one drop."

"Very well." The gentleman smiled. "Well, I guess you're wondering what your new duties with our marvelous organization will entail."

"I guess you can say I was somewhat wondering why I was snatched from my car at an intersection and brought to this hell hole of a place," Joshua said in a terse voice. "And I guess you can say I was wondering why I was branded with a hot iron like some damn cattle at an auction and forced to sleep in a room no bigger than a closet," he said as his voice began to rise. "Yes, Mr. Bob Kramer, I was somewhat wondering what this all means."

"Well, like I told you at your initiation into our organization yesterday, you were recruited here to be somewhat of a spokesman for Purification Of America Today," he said as he leaned back in his chair and continued his warm, welcoming smile. "You'll give the public, through your wonderful blog, a view of how this organization feels about certain issues through our point of view. You'll no longer state those liberal, godless views the way that you've been doing in the past in your blog anymore now that you're a member of Purification Of America Today."

"I never asked to be a member of Purification Of America Today," Joshua said with a sneer.

"Oh, you're going to love it," the old gentleman said with a cackle. "Just think of all the wonderful things that you're now going to be writing to all of your followers, Mr. Edwards. You're finally going to be giving this new shameful, liberal America what it really needs to hear."

"Sounds like I'm going to be censored."

"If you want to call it that."

"Wonderful," Joshua said with a deep sigh.

"But that's not all of what your duties with us will be, Mr. Edwards."

"Well, what else will my *duties*, as you call them, be?"

"There's quite an impressive list," the old gentleman said as he folded his arms. "Tomorrow, you'll be going with a couple of your new brothers to rob a bank in Cleveland. You'll be carrying an automatic M-16 rifle, not loaded of course, and you'll be our lead point man. Then the next day, you'll go with your new brothers to bomb a Jewish synagogue in Boston, and that should be really fun. And the next day after that, you'll go with your new brothers to raid a college campus as we'll pick out and kill the Muslims who attend this particular university in New York. We won't target any of the good white students, just the Muslim filth that's corrupting our good country."

Joshua stared at the head executive of Purification Of America Today in total silence as the old gentleman sat peacefully behind his desk while staring back at Joshua. There seemed to be no reservation whatsoever in the old man's demeanor. Joshua was so shocked and stunned at the words he'd just heard that he literally couldn't form any words to come out of his mouth.

"This is some kind of joke, isn't it?" Joshua finally said in a flabbergasted voice. "You've got to be kidding."

"No, it's not, Mr. Edwards," the old man said in a tranquil voice. "Our agenda is already planned."

"I can't rob no bank or do any of that other stuff," Joshua said as he stared at the old man in complete bewilderment. "That's crazy."

"Oh, if you're worried about your conscience bothering you about stealing money from a bank, don't fret, Mr. Edwards," the old man said in a relaxed voice. "The bank we'll be hitting tomorrow in Cleveland is a black-owned bank in the black part of town. A bank that a lot of your kind of people go there to cash welfare checks and other handouts that they get from the government in which they didn't work for. So robbing this particular black-owned bank will be more like taking money back that truly belongs to good honest, hardworking taxpayers."

"You're insane," Joshua said as he suddenly glared at the old man. "No way in hell will I do something like that!"

"Oh, you'll do it, Mr. Edwards," the old man said. He slowly propped his elbows on his desk and met Joshua's glare with a hot, menacing glare of his own. "You'll do it, because if you don't, we'll kill every last remaining little black bastard that we have back there. And we won't wait another second to do it. We'll do it right now."

"You'll what?"

"You heard what I said, Mr. Edwards," he said with the menacing eyes of a deadly viper. "You heard every single word."

Joshua's glare slowly began to melt the longer he stared at the old man's face. The old man's eyes were more terrifying and sadistic than a rattlesnake, and the longer Joshua stared at those cold, menacing eyes, he began to fear that the deadly snake would attack.

"Well, now that we have your agenda set for the next few days," the old man suddenly said once again in a pleasant voice, "let's begin with our next interview."

The old man opened the drawer to his desk and pulled out a notepad and a pen. One of the huge brutes, who stood guard by the office door, immediately went and grabbed the notepad and pen from the old man and took the items to Joshua. Joshua gave the head executive of Purification Of America Today a befuddled look as the old man smiled at him and nodded toward the pen and pad. Knowing that protesting at this particular moment would be foolish to do, Joshua slowly took the pad and pen from the huge brute.

"Now, today, we'll be talking about a serious social issue that we here at Purification Of America Today believe is beginning to take this country down to the depths of corruption, and that's the issue of men marrying men and women marrying women. However, the liberals in this country like to call it marriage equality," the old man said as he once again leaned back in his chair. "So, let's begin our conversation, shall we."

Joshua sat at a desk in a room with a laptop in front of him. A bodyguard, posted inside the room, watched him carefully as he wrote the second draft of the editorial on marriage equality that he would insert into his blog, Justice For All.

Just as their deal had stated before, if Joshua wrote a rebuttal to an interview in his blog, a kidnapped child would be set free, and Kramer promised that the deal still applied. Joshua, however, was now being censored, and the first draft that he showed for approval for entry into his blog was thoroughly rejected.

The head executive of Purification Of America Today forced Joshua to write another draft that better suited their organization's viewpoint concerning the topic at hand. Joshua knew he had to get the second draft correct, because if he didn't, Bob Kramer had already promised that one of the kids being held hostage would have to pay for it with his or her life.

When Joshua's second draft finally got approved by the old man, Joshua was allowed to log into his blog from the laptop. Under the watchful eye of his bodyguard hovering over him, Joshua entitled his new blog entry, A Special Message To All Americans. Joshua literally felt rotten as he stared at the title, but he knew he simply had no choice whatsoever:

A Special Message To All Americans

Hello, people of America. I'm now a certified blood member of Purification Of America Today. As a certified blood member of this wonderful organization, I would like to state my views on a degenerate, depraved culture that is corrupting this country, and that is the culture of homosexuality.

What used to be reserved for the closet for the most sexually depraved individuals in this country has now become a public bedroom for everyone in America to see. Our laws, our culture, and our entire way of life have become twisted by a perverted movement that has taken over our government, our schools, and our social networks.

The LGBT community has created a cancerous effect of staggering proportions that has rippled throughout the entire country. They are at the forefront of all the pains and ails that are plaguing our society. We, as a nation, must find a way to purify the smudge and filth that this corrupt community has infiltrated upon the minds of our precious youth. As long as this movement is able to continue to disseminate the degraded, immoral values that it's spreading on a daily basis, this country will continue to implode and suffocate from its own puke at an astonishing rate.

The people of America must come together to halt this wicked movement in its tracks and prevent it from spreading any further. Marriage equality is nothing but poison that is corroding the social fabric of this great nation. A union of laws and the code of decency have been usurped by this depraved, sinister movement over the years and have made a mockery of all of our lives. They have won the battle, but this misguided movement must not win the war. The LGBT movement must be eliminated, and it must be vanquished before it completely stains the integrity of this nation.

This is the viewpoint of Joshua Edwards, the newly inducted blood brother of Purification Of America Today.

After Joshua had submitted his column into his blog, Justice For All, he was escorted back to his sleeping quarters by his guard and once again locked inside the cramped, stuffy room. Joshua slowly went to his bunk and stretched out on the hard, uncomfortable cot.

As Joshua rested on his cot staring at the ceiling, he felt horrible about what he'd just written and submitted into his blog. He knew there was going to be a world of backlash coming his way for writing such an incendiary column, but he knew his followers, if they didn't already know he'd been kidnapped by Purification Of America Today, had to know that he was being censored and blackmailed. He'd been too much of a progressive minded journalist over the years in his award winning blog and in his bestselling books that he'd written to state such harsh rhetoric. It just wasn't his forte, and it definitely wasn't his journalistic style.

All of that, however, didn't matter at the moment. What really troubled his mind as he lay there staring at the ceiling was his agenda for tomorrow. The prospect of being a part of a bank robbery seemed so outlandish and surreal to even be true. Joshua, despite his stern objections to even contemplate going along with such an unlawful endeavor, knew that a gun was virtually being held, not to his own head, but to the head of every one of those innocent little kids currently being held hostage.

He knew, as bad as his options seemed, that if he didn't go along with what he was ordered to do, the eighty-six-year-old head executive of Purification Of America Today was crazy and sinister enough to indeed order the murder of one those kids. The thought of that prospect was just too much for him to bear.

So as Joshua lay there in his tight, cramped room staring at the ceiling, he knew there was no way out. He simply had no choice; he had to go along with the devil's plan to prevent the slaughter of an innocent, precious child.

Chapter 20

Joshua sat inside a van parked near First Union Bank in Cleveland as his legs wouldn't stop shaking. He was more nervous than he'd been in his life. He and four other members of Purification Of America Today were dressed in all black with automatic M-16 rifles clutched in their hands. His comrades' M-16 rifles were fully loaded and ready to fire, but Joshua's rifle was totally empty. Joshua knew he was only there to show the entire world that he'd truly been inducted into the brotherhood of Purification Of America Today. More than likely, though, he knew he was just being used to make a mockery of and to further the goals of this twisted, evil terrorist organization.

"Alright, boys, it's time to do this," one of the men said as he looked around at his comrades inside the van. "Joe, you take care of those money drawers up front while Frank, you and Eddie hit the vault. And you, *Mr. Joshua Edwards*," he said with a sneer, "you're our point man and you know what to do. I'm going to be keeping an eye on you the entire time. If you screw up or try to make a move to escape, you're going to be lying dead on the floor of that bank. Understand?"

Joshua nervously looked around at the gun toting men inside the van. Sweat was already starting to pour down his face. "No one inside that bank is going to get harmed, correct?" he said with fear dancing in his eyes. "You promised no one would be hurt, right?"

"The only one who's going to get blasted inside that bank is you, Edwards, if you screw up!" he yelled as he glared at him like fire. "You and every last little black bastard that's still back at the compound. So you just remember that."

Joshua closed his eyes and slowly nodded.

"Alright," the man said when he looked around at everyone. "Let's do this."

The men suddenly donned black masks to cover their faces. Joshua was the only one who didn't have a mask to put on. He knew this was by design. He knew Purification Of America Today wanted the entire world to see his face and know that he was now a certified bank robber.

Joshua and his fellow bank robbers exited the van and made a quick dash down the sidewalk for the bank. Each step that Joshua took toward the bank, his legs began to feel as weak as rubber. It felt like he was stepping into deep quick sand. In fact, Joshua hoped he'd just sink into the abyss of the sidewalk and totally disappear forever.

When Joshua and his fellow bank robbers entered the First Union Bank, the robbers with the loaded M-16 rifles fired their weapons toward the ceiling. All the people in the bank immediately hit the floor in terrified panic. The robbers quickly subdued the lone bank guard, took his weapon, and forced him to the ground. The entire bank was now at their mercy.

"Alright, this is a raid!" Joshua announced to everyone on the bank floor in a nervous, shaky voice as he held his empty M-16 rifle limp in his hand. "We, the brothers of Purification Of America Today, have come to take back all the money that you shiftless, no account niggers have stolen from the government."

While three of the bank robbers quickly began taking all the money from the teller drawers and the vault of the bank, Joshua stood nervously in the middle of the bank and surveyed the entire scene.

As the robbery took place, Joshua slowly scanned the frightened, terrified faces of all the people lying on the floor. Some of the people stared nervously back at him, trembling and shaking.

Joshua felt utterly terrible as he gazed at the people staring at him with total fear in their eyes. He felt like a stone cold criminal of the highest order. The way he felt, he thought at any second that he was going to pass out and collapse onto the floor. He wanted to run out of the bank as fast as he could and flee the scene, but when he slowly turned to glance at his rear, he saw one of his Purification Of America Today brothers standing guard by the door with his M-16 rifle leveled dead at his back.

When the three robbers raiding the bank teller drawers and the bank vault had finally collected a substantial amount of loot, the thieves left the terrified people lying on the floor as they fled the bank and made their getaway.

That night Faye was literally about to go out of her mind. She paced the floor of her bedroom back and forth in a frantic manner while the evening news played on her widescreen TV.

The top story of the night was the bank robbery in Cleveland. Purification Of America Today had struck again, but this time they had a new addition to their organization. Joshua Edwards, the famed author of the blog, Justice For All, who'd been kidnapped only days ago, was shown on the bank camera of the First Union Bank in Cleveland, OH wielding an M-16 assault rifle as he held up the bank. The breaking news reported around the country was literally incredible. It was like the famed Patty Hearst incident happening all over again, and reporters had a field day with it.

The news was utterly devastating to Faye. Reporters and friends were constantly calling her, wanting to get an on the spot interview about the situation or wanting to get her feelings and opinions about what transpired. All the constant calls were nerve wracking. It made her feel as if her nerves were being squeezed through a shredder and her mind was being tossed in a blender.

Faye was worried sick that Purification Of America Today was going harm her husband. They were obviously blackmailing him to do unspeakable criminal acts, forcing him to write the most vile, heinous rhetoric in his blog to suit their objectives, and it was no telling what else they had in store for him. Faye knew the authorities had to rescue Joshua before it was too late. She feared it was only a matter of time before Purification Of America Today would ultimately kill him.

When Faye suddenly heard the doorbell ring, she quickly headed down the winding staircase, scampered through the foyer, and answered her front door. Two FBI agents Faye had recognized who'd come to the house on a previous occasion stood on her porch. She had suspected that the FBI would probably show up. The gravity of the situation under which her husband was entangled required immediate attention.

"Mrs. Edwards, Agent Dale Gatewood and Agent Sam Elliott here," he said when she opened the door. "We need to speak to you once again concerning your husband."

"Yes, please, come in," Faye quickly said. The men entered the foyer of the house as she escorted them to the parlor. "Please, have a seat."

"Mrs. Edwards, I know this is a difficult time for you," he said as he and his partner had a seat on a couch while Faye sat on a sofa across from them. "I know you're probably upset about what's going on, but I assure you, the Federal Bureau of Investigation is doing everything that it possibly can to try to locate where Purification Of America Today is currently holding your husband."

"Officers, that bank robbery happened in Cleveland," she said in an uneasy voice. "They have to be holding my husband somewhere around the vicinity of that city. They *must* be holding him somewhere near there."

"Ma'am, we have over a hundred agents at this moment combing the area of Cleveland and all the surrounding areas near the city," he said in an optimistic voice. "If they're anywhere in that vicinity, we'll certainly locate them. In fact, we've already made numerous arrests of members of their affiliate chapters in other states around the country. So we're slowly, but surely, beginning to break apart their organization."

"But that's not doing my husband any damn good at the moment!" Faye lashed out as she glared at the two agents. "I'm afraid if my husband isn't rescued within the next day or so, they're going to kill him."

"We certainly realize that, and that's why we've put such large numbers of agents on the case around Cleveland to locate where Purification Of America Today is holding up at. You have to realize, this organization is pretty resourceful at moving around the country, Mrs. Edwards. They're a network that has plenty of money and they have well entrenched connections to help them. They're one of the most elusive organizations we've ever encountered."

"If they're so well financed, then why the hell are they going around robbing banks?"

"It's mere intimidation, ma'am," he said without reservation. "They're a white supremacy hate group that's trying to make a statement to all America. The institution they hit today was a black-owned bank on the black side of town. They used your husband in the robbery only to make a point and to mock and embarrass him. Obviously, they're using blackmail and coercion tactics, threatening to kill the kids that they're still holding hostage to make your husband oblige with their tactics."

"Well, I'd say it's working damn well, wouldn't you say?" she said with a hiss of anger.

"It certainly seems to be."

"Purification Of America Today always seems to be two steps ahead of the FBI all the time. All of what I keep getting from you guys is nothing but a bunch of useless promises," she said with a sigh as she began to rub her temples. "I almost hate to see what in the world they have in store for my husband tomorrow when I turn on the TV."

Faye let out a long, deep sigh. She slowly began to massage her aching temples. Her head suddenly felt as if it were about to explode into a million pieces at any second. A whole bottle of Tylenol wouldn't have stopped the pain pulsating between her temples. She needed something much stronger and powerful to stop the sheer agony pounding inside her head.

The agents had suddenly become dead silent while Faye tried to compose herself. She was in no hurry to speak to the gentlemen sitting across from her.

"So, what happens next?" she finally said in a tired, weary voice.

"Just be patient, Mrs. Edwards," the agent said in a comforting, coaxing voice. "We're going to get Purification Of America Today and put this organization away for good. And we're going to do our best to bring your husband back home, safe and sound."

"I certainly hope you can," she said in a dismal voice. "I certainly do."

The FBI agents rose to leave as Faye escorted them out of the parlor. When she let them out the front door, she headed back upstairs to her bedroom, turned off the lights and TV, and immediately crawled into bed. With her head pounding like a giant wrecking ball smashing into it and with tears streaming down her face, she tried to force all of the pain and misery from her exhausted body as she focused on nothing but Joshua's sweet, gentle face.

Joshua rested on the hard, uncomfortable cot in his tight cramped room feeling utterly terrible and miserable. Tonight he felt like a fugitive of the highest order. He was now an accomplice to a bank robbery, a villain on the run from the law. As dreadful as that was, tomorrow had the potential of being even more horrible and horrendous. Tomorrow was the day that Purification Of America Today would bomb a Jewish synagogue in Boston and kill as many people as they could.

He'd already made up his mind. There was no way on earth that he was going to go along with what Purification Of America Today had in store for him tomorrow. They would just have to kill him. While he lay staring through the darkness of his cramped room, he was already mentally preparing himself to be shot and killed at any moment for his refusal to go along with their evil, wretched plans.

The thought of those five remaining kidnapped kids, however, suddenly sent a cold shiver over Joshua's entire body. Joshua knew full well that the sadistic, eighty-six-year-old head of Purification Of America Today would very well put a bullet into the heads of all of the remaining kids still being held kidnapped if he refused to go along with their plans.

Kramer probably would even let him *personally* live just so he could witness the murder of those precious little souls and suffer the agony of seeing them die in such a cruel, merciless way. The sheer agony of living with that for the rest of his life was a torture that Joshua couldn't bear. He'd rather be shot before he'd live with the agony of watching those precious little kids die in such a despicable way.

As Joshua was about to literally go out of his mind, the small slot on the steel door of his room began to slide open. Joshua suddenly heard his name being whispered by someone on the other side of the door. Through the darkness of his room, he slowly rose from his cot and went to the door. He gazed through the small open slot on the door and immediately recognized the face on the other side. It was Mr. Z, his improbable new friend with the KILL NIGGERS tattoo engraved on his forehead.

"Edwards," the voice whispered again through the slot. "Are you listening?"

"Yeah, what is it?"

"Tonight's the night you're going to get the hell out of here."

"What, they're setting me free?"

"No, *I'm* going to help you get out of here," Mr. Z said. He quickly looked up and down the long, dark hallway. "The coast is clear right now, so tonight you're going to get your lucky break."

"What about the kids?"

"No can do, man." He quickly shook his head. "They've moved them to the other side of the compound, and two guards are stationed near their cell."

"There's no way I'm leaving here without those kids."

"Look, man, this is your chance to make a run for it," he said angrily through the slot. "You might not get this chance tomorrow night or the night after that, because you know they're eventually going to put a damn bullet in your head sooner or later."

"I ain't leaving here without those kids!" Joshua yelled through the slot. "Now, you've got to find a way to help me get those kids out of here."

"It's impossible!"

"Come on, man, you got to find a way to get those kids out of here." Joshua pleaded as he glared through the slot. "There's got to be some way."

"There ain't no way."

"Well, I'm not leaving without those kids. You can forget it."

"You're a damn fool, Edwards." Mr. Z lashed out as he kept his voice low. "I thought you were one of the smart niggers, but I guess I was wrong. When they finally kill you, I'm going to look forward to shoveling dirt over your dead, sorry ass!"

The small slot on the steel door suddenly slammed shut. Joshua desperately called for Mr. Z over and over through the door, but there was absolutely no answer. To his horror, he began to realize that his chance at freedom had slipped away and it wasn't coming back.

Joshua, with his heart broken, slowly slumped to the floor as he rested against the heavy steel door. The nightmare he'd been going through for the last several days was only continuing to get worse.

When he didn't think he'd get another chance at clemency, the small slot on the steel door once again sprung open. Joshua quickly rose from the floor and peered through the open slot; Mr. Z hadn't left, he was still there. He glared dead straight into Joshua's eyes with a look so vicious that the foul, putrid smell of hate literally stunk up the air.

"Look, Mr. Z . . . I mean Zack," Joshua said in a low, humbled voice. "I have to try to take those kids with me. I could never live with myself if I ran off and I knew those kids were still left here to be mentally tortured and abused. When I came to visit you at the jail that day, you yourself said you didn't think those kids should have to suffer and die. That's why you contacted me in the first place. You wanted to try to help save those kids, remember?"

Joshua glanced through the dark open slot while he and Mr. Z stared at one another in total silence. They stared at one another so long and so intense, it seemed as if a game of chess were at hand, and the one who looked away would capitulate to the other.

Suddenly, without saying a word, Mr. Z slammed the slot shut once again. When Joshua knew that his new, improbable friend had gone and wasn't coming back, he slowly went back to his hard, uncomfortable cot. As he stretched out on his bed of nails and spikes, he stared through the darkness of his holding cell hoping for a miracle.

He and those helpless little kids needed a break. They desperately needed some kind of miracle to go their way.

About an hour later when he'd nearly dozed off to sleep, Joshua began to hear the sound of a key rattling inside the lock of the door. Seconds later, the heavy steel door swung open. Joshua saw that it was Mr. Z; he'd suddenly come back.

"Let's go," Mr. Z said as he glared at Joshua lying on the cot. "I've already taken care of one of the guards who was on duty by the kids' holding cell. So, now, we only have one guard left to deal with."

Joshua quickly rose from the cot and followed Mr. Z as they headed out of his holding cell. They began to walk briskly down a long corridor as they headed to the other side of the compound.

"What do you mean, you took care of one of the guards?" Joshua asked fearfully as he followed Mr. Z.

"I let him have my night with Doris and I took his place guarding the compound and the kids' cell tonight."

"Doris?"

"Doris Minford," he said as they kept walking. "She's a prostitute Mr. Kramer sometimes flies in to oblige all the boys of our organization from time to time."

"Only one prostitute for all the men here?"

"You've never spent a night with Doris," he said in a reserved voice. "Doris is better than a dozen good prostitutes put together."

Mr. Z suddenly stopped at a storage closet, opened it, and grabbed a hammer. With the hammer firmly in his hand, he kept walking down the corridor until he came to the end of a corner. He slowly peeked around the corner while Joshua stood virtually hugged to his back.

With his finger pressed to his lips telling Joshua to stay as quiet as possible, Mr. Z motioned for Joshua to follow him around the corner. A guard sat in a chair next to a holding cell with his back turned, reading a magazine. Mr. Z sneaked up on the guard, and with the force of a sledge hammer, gave the guard a vicious whack across the back of his head with the hammer. The guard tumbled out of his chair and fell face-first to the floor unconscious.

Without wasting a second, Mr. Z quickly reached down and snatched the cell key ring from the guard's pants belt. He took the key ring and unlocked the holding cell. Mr. Z and Joshua dashed into the holding cell and quickly roused the four sleeping kids in the room. The kids looked totally alarmed and petrified, but they remained silent when Mr. Z suddenly pressed his finger to his lips once again, indicating for them to remain silent.

"You're going home, kids," he whispered to all the kids in the room. "Just remain totally silent and follow us."

"Hey, there are only four kids here," Joshua suddenly whispered to Mr. Z with alarm in his voice. "There's supposed to be five kids. What happened to the other kid?"

"Kramer had one released early this morning after you wrote that blog the other day on homos and lesbians, remember?"

"Ah, yes," Joshua said with a sneer as he shook his head in complete frustration. "The good, honest Mr. Bob Kramer and our wonderful little deal. How could I ever forget?"

When they'd finally gotten the kids up and dressed, they led them out of the holding cell and quickly led them down the corridor to the back of the compound. They opened a back door and hurried outside. Three different vans were parked in the back. Mr. Z pointed to a green van for Joshua and the four kids to get into as they quickly piled in. Joshua got in on the driver's side and rolled down the window as Mr. Z handed him the keys.

"Where are we exactly?" Joshua asked in a nervous voice.

"You're about twenty miles before you hit the nearest freeway. Just peel rubber out of here, turn right, and keep driving until you come to the nearest interstate. Hop onto that interstate and it'll take you west."

"West, straight to California?"

Mr. Z nodded.

Joshua looked at his improbable friend for a quick second. "Well, so long my good friend. I think you're going to have to get you a new tattoo," he said as he gazed at his forehead, "because that one doesn't suit you anymore."

Joshua put the key into the ignition, started the van, and took off as he left the compound like a streak of lightning.

Chapter 21

Joshua had driven all the way to Kansas City before he finally decided he'd gotten far enough away from the compound in Ohio. The entire time he sped across the heartland of America, he was petrified that someone from Purification Of America Today was going to come chasing him during the middle of the night. He'd been driving like a manic zombie on the road for the past eleven hours. Now, daylight and nearly seven hundred miles had become his best ally to thwart the scent of his potential pursuers.

After coming to a stop in Kansas City, Joshua went straight to the police as he turned over the four kids he carried with him into their custody. Joshua was totally relieved that he'd finally gotten the kids who'd been kidnapped for so many weeks returned to safety. He was more than thankful and grateful that Mr. Z had helped him and those innocent little children escape from the nightmare of that compound. What he did took a lot of courage and guts to go against his organization's wishes, however misguided and evil as they were. Joshua was even worried for his new friend's safety. The type of cruel, vicious animals that Purification Of America Today were, he knew they'd have no problem whatsoever at eating and devouring their own kind.

When Joshua delivered the four remaining kids to the authorities in

Kansas City, the FBI immediately seized him and took him into custody. For endless hours, he was probed and interrogated on his wild, whirlwind stint over the last several days with Purification Of America Today.

Joshua revealed to the FBI everything he knew. He revealed the organization's plans to bomb a Jewish synagogue in Boston, to their desires to kill Muslims on a college university campus in New York. That valuable information was thoroughly interrogated and questioned, but what the FBI really grilled Joshua for hours and hours on was his involvement with the bank robbery in Cleveland.

Suspecting all along that Joshua had been forced to go along with the bank robbery, especially when video footage of the camera inside the bank clearly showed that one of the members of Purification Of America Today held an M-16 rifle at his back from a distance, the FBI still had to officially clear Joshua of any criminal activity that he'd been involved in. The process was long and arduous, particularly when it came to all the formalities and red tape that the FBI had to go through.

Finally, after three days of relentless questioning and probing, the FBI decided not to bring any charges against Joshua for his involvement in the First Union Bank robbery in Cleveland. They concluded that he'd been forcefully indoctrinated into the organization of Purification Of America Today and was forced to commit the criminal undertaking under extreme threat and duress.

Chapter 22

Joshua was suddenly more popular and in demand than any Hollywood actor. A week after his horrendous ordeal from escaping from the compound in Ohio, he'd done a plethora of national television talk shows and had given dozens of interviews to countless reporters.

The entire nation wanted to hear every detail of Joshua's disturbing, traumatic time being forced to be a blood member of Purification Of America Today, his experience being forced to rob a bank, and the story of how he escaped from that Ohio compound with those kidnapped kids. Joshua was so in demand, he was like an overloaded switchboard as an operator went crazy trying to plug in and connect all the requests to speak with him. He became so busy that he had to attain the services of a publicist to arrange his time properly. Reporters and journalists who wanted to have a conversation with him, literally had to pick an appointed time slot to gain access to his time.

While Joshua became the news media superstar that the entire country desperately wanted to see and hear from, the Federal Bureau of Investigation began to make inroads in dismantling the organization of Purification Of America Today.

All twelve regional chapters in Iowa, Montana, Texas, Washington,

Idaho, Oklahoma, and California had been completely eradicated. Over a thousand organizational members of Purification Of America Today had been arrested and indicted on charges ranging from murder, acts of bombing, kidnapping, conspiracy to take over the government, and other assorted hate crimes that had violated the rights of American citizens. Their base had now been completely eviscerated and destroyed, and fortunately, no Jewish synagogues, college campuses, nor any other acts of terror had since been committed by their organization.

The threat, however, hadn't been completely neutralized. The twelve highest ranking members of Purification Of America Today, along with their eighty-six-year-old leader, hadn't been arrested and brought to justice. Authorities had found the compound in Ohio that the organization had last been residing in, but when they finally got there, the place had been vacated.

The twelve highest ranking members of the organization and their leader had fled the compound and were now on the run. With no more known places of residence around the country to hide their operations, federal authorities knew it was only a matter of time before they completely reined in the rest of the organization. Until they were all under lock and key, however, Purification Of America Today remained a major threat, and America was still very much in danger.

Chapter 23

Joshua and Faye were at home sitting at their kitchen table eating dinner as they discussed each other's agenda. It felt totally wonderful and exhilarating to be back in the company with one another after being flung apart under such egregious, tumultuous circumstances. Joshua was so thrilled to finally be free of Purification Of America Today and to have accomplished his mission of rescuing those innocent kids held kidnapped for so long, that he could've literally kissed the ground under him. It truly felt like manna falling from heaven; a rainbow was definitely hovering over his presence.

There were still problems, however. The most pressing problem that Joshua had to deal with since returning home from his imprisonment, was dealing with the aftermath of his latest entry to his blog, Justice For All, that Purification Of America Today had forced him to write during his captivity.

The blog entry, A Special Message To All Americans, had created a storm of controversy, not only in the LGBT community, but in other news cycles throughout the country. Various groups and organizations that were highly offended by Joshua's harsh rhetoric began to protest Joshua's blog. They demanded that Joshua explain his divisive rhetoric before the television cameras and give a public apology. Some were even demanding a total ban entirely of his blog, Justice For All, for creating such a firestorm across social circles throughout the country.

One of the leading organizations at the forefront calling for a total ban of Joshua's blog was his own daughter's lesbian-supported Internet blog, New Day. It vehemently called for Joshua to stand before the LGBT community and answer for the cruel, vicious message that he'd spread so haphazardly in his highly followed blog. Everyone wanted and demanded answers, and they wanted it right away.

Joshua got his opportunity to answer for what he'd written when he was invited to attend a special political summit tonight in Los Angeles that the LGBT community was giving to present their upcoming platform to their constituent base. Wanting desperately to state his view and testify on his own behalf, Joshua gladly accepted the invitation. He was finally going to set the record straight.

"What time does your plane leave tomorrow morning for New York?" Joshua asked Faye as they ate at the kitchen table.

"Eight in the morning," Faye said. She poured herself another glass of tea. "It's a long five hour flight to New York. I'll have a little time to check into the hotel and get a little rest before the conference starts tomorrow evening."

"How many national conferences does this make now for your organization that you've gone to?"

"I started A Hand In Need ten years ago, so this makes our sixth national conference that we've had."

"How many members does your organization have nationally now?"

"I believe we've grown to nearly a hundred thousand."

"That's quite impressive," Joshua said with a generous smile.

"Indeed, it is," she said, returning his smile.

The TV in the kitchen was on the world news as Joshua and Faye watched as they ate dinner. The state of the economy, wildfires in California, and the Pope's visit to America seemed to occupy the slate of tonight's news. It was the first evening that Joshua's heroic escape from the compound in Ohio, the story of the kidnapped kids, or the ongoing hunt for the remaining members of Purification Of America Today didn't dominate the entirety of the news.

"What time are you heading downtown for that summit meeting tonight?"

"I'll leave when the news goes off."

"You know they're going to tear you apart at that meeting," Faye said giving him a hard look. "You know that, don't you?"

"Maybe so," Joshua said with a sigh. "But I must make them, and the entire LGBT community, realize that I was pressured to write what I wrote in my blog while I was in that hell hole. Purification Of America Today was literally going to kill one of those children if I didn't state those views."

"I don't think that's going to soften the vitriol and the rage that's going to be flung your way tonight," Faye said, shaking her head. "They're going to be out for your blood."

"You want to take up the shield and go in my place?"

"I don't think so, sweetheart," Faye said with a mocking smile. "It's your blood they want, not mine. Besides, I have some more packing to do tonight before my plane leaves for New York tomorrow morning."

"Sure you do."

"Oh, and you know Tyesha is going to be one of the panelists on that summit tonight?"

"Say what?" Joshua said in an alarmed voice.

"She called this morning," Faye said in an ominous voice. "Her exact words she wanted me to tell you was that she couldn't wait until tonight so she can finally grill your black ass."

"That's just perfect." Joshua slowly closed his eyes and let out a deep, agonizing moan. "Just perfect."

The phone suddenly rang. Faye rose from the kitchen table to answer it. When she did, she slowly handed the phone to Joshua as she gave him another ominous look.

"Is it a reporter?"

"Far worse."

Joshua took the phone. "Hello?"

"Josh."

Joshua immediately closed his eyes and sighed when he heard Conrad's voice. He almost would've rather heard the voice of Bob Kramer himself than to hear from his obnoxious, intolerable brother.

"What the hell do you want?"

"Look, Josh, why don't you drop by so we can have us a little talk," Conrad said in an easy, caring voice. "We haven't had a chance to talk since you've been through your terrible ordeal and all. You know, no matter what went down with us at that restaurant that night, we're still brothers," he said affectionately. "So, if there's anything you want to get off your chest, you can come by and talk about it. It might help you feel better."

Joshua silently held the phone limp in his hand for a couple of seconds. He couldn't believe what he heard. Conrad had never shown any true brotherly affection toward him. It had always been a tug of war between them; a race for the first one to cross the finish line.

"So, you want me to come by your house tomorrow evening so we can talk?"

"Well, no. I'll be at the radio station working a little late tomorrow evening. So why don't you just drop by here at Sunset 101 around six and we can talk for a while."

"You want me to drop by the radio station so we can talk?"

"Yeah."

"Man, you ain't fooling me one bit!" Joshua suddenly said in a steamed voice. "You just want me to come on the radio show tomorrow evening so you can grill me on how my harrowing experience was being kidnapped by Purification Of America Today. You got a slick way of trying to ask me to come on the radio show just so you can get a damn ratings bonanza off of me. Man, you're truly the pits!"

"Well, hell, you've done nearly every other TV and radio show that there is across the damn country since you've been released." Conrad fired back in a hostile voice. "Why not do my radio show? Is there something wrong with helping family out?"

"You know, for a split second, I thought you truly cared about my well-being," Joshua said as his rage began to build. "But you wouldn't give a damn if those bastards would've put a bullet into my head and tossed me off a bridge. As long as you can say to your radio listeners that you're the brother to the poor dead bastard, your world is just fine!"

Joshua hung up the phone as his anger simmered over.

"Trouble in the Edward family?" Faye said facetiously.

"That fat bastard!"

The phone suddenly began to ring again. Joshua quickly picked it up.

"What is it?" he yelled into the receiver.

"Dad, I'm in jail," Kahila's deep voice came blaring through. "I've been arrested."

"Arrested?"

"Yeah."

"What happened?"

"Well, me and about thirty other members of the Black Unity Coalition were protesting all of this unwarranted police arrests of some our members that the police have been doing lately. We were in front of the downtown L.A. police station protesting when these damn racist skinheads all of a sudden showed up and started harassing us. Well, I had my gun on me, so I pulled it out and started firing it into the air to let them know what they were up against."

"Did anybody get shot?"

"No. But I was arrested for firing off my gun recklessly and causing a public disturbance."

"Oh, good heavens, Kahila," Joshua said in an exasperated voice. "How in the world could you go around carrying a gun and firing it off like some crazy lunatic? Boy, your damn record isn't squeaky clean, you know."

"I don't have no damn record to speak of," Kahila said as he shot back.

"Yeah, that's because I've been hiring all these lawyers over the years to keep getting your tail out of trouble!" Joshua suddenly yelled. Not wanting to get too upset, he began to calm down. "Alright, sit tight," he finally said in a controlled voice. "I'll see about getting you out."

Joshua hung up the phone and looked at Faye.

"That was Kahila. He's been—"

"I heard," she said in a somber voice.

"You don't seem too upset."

"After the nerve-wracking hellish experience that I just went through dealing with your situation, I said that I wasn't going to give myself any more near heart attacks again," she said with a deep sigh. "So, what are you going to do?"

"Well, it's getting late. I better head on to this summit meeting," Joshua said while he slid on his suit coat. "Then after it's over, I'll go by the downtown jail and see if I can get Kahila out."

"Don't fret about it too much," Faye said in a loving voice as she began to fix his necktie. "Just look at this way. It's much better than being kidnapped and forced to rob a bank, now isn't it?"

"I'm beginning to wonder if it really is," he said with a chuckle.

Joshua gave Faye a gentle kiss, then he left the kitchen and headed out the front door.

Joshua sat alone at a small table on a stage as a table of four panelists faced him five feet away. A crowd of about five hundred was in attendance in the convention hall as the event was televised locally around the L.A. area. Joshua was being pelted with a series of questions on the topic of his recent entry to his blog, Justice For All. The questions being fired at him came like fiery arrows from a pack of Apache Indians who'd come for the kill, but Joshua held the fort down as best as he could and kept his cavalry from being slaughtered.

"Mr. Edwards, we realize that you were being held kidnapped by Purification Of America Today when you wrote your latest entry to your blog," Jill Anderson, head of the popular lesbian magazine, *Flourishing In The Twenty First Century*, said when she directed her question to Joshua. "However, you stated some very degrading, demeaning opinions directed toward the LGBT community that we very much took offense to. Now that you're no longer held in captivity and are no longer being blackmailed, how do you personally feel about the LGBT community?"

"I feel that the LGBT community deserves the same rights and privileges that all Americans enjoy," Joshua said eloquently into his microphone as the camera was on him. "I equate what the LGBT community has gone through over the last several years as equal to what the African American community went through during the civil rights movement. The LGBT community's struggle for equality is every American's struggle for equality."

"So do you have any reservations for what the LGBT community stands for?"

"No, I don't."

"Mr. Edwards," another panelist asked, "why did you describe the LGBT community as a depraved, degenerate culture that's corrupting our country?"

"Once again, the words that were produced in the latest entry to my blog were not my true words," Joshua said in a heartfelt voice. "Those words were virtually dictated to me by an evil, twisted organization that wanted nothing but to create anarchy and chaos throughout the entire country. Purification Of America Today are the ones who are depraved and degenerate, and they're corrupting this country."

"Is that your way of apologizing for your words, Mr. Edwards?"

"Profoundly it is," Joshua said into the microphone. "I cannot state how sorry I am for those misguided words that I'm ashamed to even say that I was forced to put into my blog."

"Mr. Edwards, will you help with various causes, benefits, and charities that the LGBT community is trying to promote to help further awareness of what our community is trying to accomplish?" another panelist asked. "You could be a tremendous asset for the LGBT community considering the level of people you reach with your blog on a weekly basis."

"Yes, I am."

"Are you willing to personally help with certain benefits and charities out of your own pocket?" the panelist asked with a dubious look. "In other words, Mr. Edwards, are willing to put your money where your mouth is?"

"Indeed I am," Joshua said with a nod. "In fact, I'm ready to write a check in the amount of fifty thousand dollars to any worthwhile charity that the LGBT community deems will further the goals of its community."

A loud hubbub began to suddenly brew around the convention hall as a hearty applause broke out. Joshua slowly smiled when the people in the audience began to stand while they continued to clap. It seemed that his worst fears of those fiery arrows being aimed at him were finally over.

"Mr. Edwards, I have a question for you," his daughter, who sat at the panel table, suddenly said into her microphone as the applause began to die away. "What is your view on marriage equality?"

Joshua stared at Tyesha across from him at the other panel table for a couple seconds, trying to compose his answer as carefully and thoughtfully as he could. He knew Tyesha was getting ready to lay into him with several more incisive questions to try to trap him. It was that intense, penetrating way in which she glared at him that made him suddenly feel the heat of those fiery arrows once again. He'd definitely seen that look in Tyesha numerous times in the past when she wanted to be wayward and rebellious.

"Well, down in my deepest soul, I believe that a marriage should be between a man and a woman," Joshua said in a careful voice. "But since our country has now adopted that marriage can legally exist between two people who want to unite, no matter their sex, then I fully support the law and the full equality of any married couple."

"Do you have any friends you associate with who are married to the same sex?"

"No, I don't."

"Tell me, Mr. Edwards, why did you come to this gathering this evening?"

"Well, I wanted to state my true opinions of how I feel about the LGBT community," Joshua said in a sincere voice as he looked at Tyseha. "I realize that the words that I was forced to write in my blog a couple of days ago were offensive to a lot of people, and I wanted to apologize."

"Because of what was written in your blog?"

"Yes."

"I see. So this is really just some publicity stunt for you to appear humble and contrite before the cameras to try to gain points and legitimize your precious award winning blog once again, isn't it?" Tyesha said in a defensive voice. "You truly don't care about the concerns and issues of what our community is trying to achieve."

"That's not true."

"Mr. Edwards, in a previous blog of yours some years ago, you thoroughly supported Proposition 8 which eliminated the rights of same-sex couples to marry here in the State of California. Do you remember that?"

"Yes, I remember."

"Do you remember the words that you wrote in that particular blog concerning your support for Proposition 8?"

"No, not exactly."

"Well, let me refresh your memory, Mr. Edwards," Tyesha said when she pulled out a sheet paper. "You stated in your blog a couple of years back entitled Support For Proposition 8 that marriage equality needs to be prevented from becoming the law of this state at all cost. California must set the example for the entire country and not let the LGBT movement win the war that it is trying to win with their agenda of marriage equality," Tyesha said as she gave Joshua a defiant look. "Sounds somewhat similar to what you said in your recent blog entry, A Special Message To All Americans, only without the colorful language, doesn't it, Mr. Edwards?"

"That's nowhere near the same as what I was forced to write during my captivity with Purification Of America Today," Joshua said defensively. "I totally refute that accusation."

"I believe it's the same," Tyesha said like a cracking whip into her microphone. "So, Mr. Edwards, how can you sit here and state that you're a supporter of our cause?"

"Years have passed since then," Joshua said apprehensively. "A person can evolve over time and come around to change views on certain issues."

"Based on your previous writings, I don't think you've changed your views one bit, Mr. Edwards," Tyesha said in a stinging voice. "In fact,

I think you're nothing but a total phony. You're a phony who's only using this forum to further your objectives."

"I resent that accusation."

"And we resent your phony ass for even showing up at this conference and telling your lies," Tyesha said in a heartless, stinging voice. "I believe I speak for everyone in the LGBT community when we all say that you and your precious blog can go take a flying leap off a damn cliff, Mr. Edwards!"

Shocked gasps and stunned expressions suddenly reverberated around the convention hall. There wasn't a silent voice anywhere.

When the summit meeting had finally concluded, the panelists and other assorted people within the media were backstage socializing. After giving a few interviews with a couple of reporters, Joshua suddenly broke away from the group of reporters surrounding him as he made his way over to Tyesha and Patricia when he spotted them.

Tyesha and Patricia had just finished talking to a group of people when they suddenly departed, and Joshua finally saw an opportunity to speak with them alone. The look on Tyesha's face when Joshua began to approach her and Patricia was like the look of a rattlesnake. The vicious rattlesnake was preparing to sink its fangs into the unwanted varmint suddenly invading their territory.

"Now, before you blow a gasket, I just wanted to say a few things," Joshua said in an easy voice when he slowly approached Tyesha and Patricia.

"I think I'm going to leave you two alone to talk," Patricia said as she began to walk away.

"No, please don't leave." Joshua quickly stopped her. "This concerns the both of you."

Patricia hesitantly stayed as the three stood silently staring at one another.

"Well?" Tyesha said impatiently while she glared at Joshua.

"Look, this is a little uncomfortable for me, I must admit," Joshua said in an uneasy voice. "The fact is, what you said out there on that stage tonight was true, Tyesha. Well, at least most of it was," he said, eying his daughter.

"I've never truly understood your perspective the way that you wanted to live your life, Tyesha," he said when he continued. "In fact, I've never really tried to understand the LGBT community at all, only in theory of being a progressive liberal person who states that I must accept certain things in the playbook to be called a progressive liberal."

"Oh, really," Tyesha said sarcastically, folding her arms.

"Well, yes. But now I want to put all of those label type things aside for good and just view you as the daughter whom I truly love. Whatever makes you happy is what I want for my daughter. And now that Patricia is part of your life permanently, I want to truly extend my love to you and Patricia and wish you nothing but the best."

When Joshua became silent when his words trailed off, the three of them just stood there as their eyes suddenly began to glance toward the floor. The silence seemed to go on forever. It seemed that not another word would be spoken. Even a faint sound or a slight sigh would've probably caused an alarm bell to screech out.

"Well, I guess if that's your way of apologizing for a lifetime full of mistakes," Tyesha suddenly said as she looked up, "I guess I should be a good sport and accept it."

Joshua gradually began to raise his head, meeting Tyesha's eyes. After a long uncomfortable moment staring at one another, Joshua slowly began to break into a small smile as Tyesha, slowly, did likewise.

When their smiles slowly began to grow, Joshua extended his arms and embraced his daughter. It was a hug that Tyesha didn't reject as she let her father cuddle and squeeze her tightly. Finally, after giving Tyesha a warm, endearing embrace, Joshua extended his arms and gave Patricia a warm hug also.

"Well, Faye and I would love to have you and Patricia over for dinner this Sunday," Joshua said in a warm voice. "Will we be expecting you two?"

Tyesha looked at Joshua for a couple seconds, then slowly nodded.

"Very well," he said with a warm smile.

Joshua gave both Tyesha and Patricia a parting soft peck on the cheek. After giving his farewell kisses, he turned and headed on his way.

Joshua finally arrived at the downtown Los Angeles jail near midnight as he sought his son's release. After having to wait an agonizing two whole hours for the process to be completed, he was at last able to post Kahila's bail. When his son was finally released, he and Kahila headed out of the jail together as they got into Joshua's new car and drove away.

The car ride through the nighttime streets of L.A. was a quiet, silent affair. There was no radio and certainly no conversation. Neither father nor son had a single thing to say to the other. There was nothing but complete, utter silence.

"Well, the least you can say is thanks for coming down to the jail and bailing me out," Joshua finally said in an angry huff while he drove. "A little gratitude for what someone has taken the time to do for you would be much appreciated."

Kahila remained silent as they rode on. "Yeah, thanks," he finally said in a dry, uninspired voice while he continued staring out of his passenger window.

"You know, in your twenty-three years, you've made getting arrested and going to jail a vocation of yours," Joshua said with malice. "And over the years, I've certainly paid my share of your tuition, if you want to call it that, just so you could continue to practice your wonderful, esteemed vocation."

"Well, I guess lately you've been trying to enter this *wonderful, esteemed* vocation yourself, haven't you?" Kahila said with spite when he turned and glared at Joshua. "You and big brother Conrad getting arrested that night in that fine, upstanding Beverly Hills restaurant in that hellish fight you two got into can certainly get you started in this wonderful vocation. Can't it?"

"Boy, don't get flippant with me."

"Oh, sorry, Father," he suddenly said with a sarcastic chuckle. "I forgot that you don't want the world to know that the author of the highly prestigious blog, Justice For All, has a new vocation that he's trying to pursue that happens to be behind bars."

Joshua and Kahila continued to ride through the night streets in total silence. The silence was so thick that neither Kahila nor Joshua would turn the slightest to even glimpse at the other. It was like the cold war was still in effect; two opposing nations that had extreme grievances with one another wouldn't acknowledge that the other even existed.

"Look, Kahila," Joshua suddenly said with a deep sigh. "Maybe we should drop the barrier that's been between us all of these years and just try to talk to one another," he said as he tried to extend an olive branch. "Can we agree to do that?"

Kahila remained totally silent.

"Whatever," he finally said after a couple of minutes.

"Kahila, I know that you've carried around a lot of resentment toward me for a number of years because I sent you off to boarding school when you were growing up," Joshua said while he kept his eyes focused on the traffic ahead. "And maybe I was wrong to send you away when you needed a father all of those years."

"Yes, you were." Kahila suddenly snapped.

"I agree. I was wrong," Joshua said in a heartfelt voice. "But, Kahila, we all make mistakes. You have to understand I was dealing with coming off my own internal problems, and your mother and I were trying to mend our relationship back together. I just thought, with as wild and loose as you were growing up at that young age, that I didn't have the mental stamina to try to raise you properly like I should. Boarding school seemed like an easy out for me at the time."

"Do you realize how it was going to school with nothing but a bunch of little rich ass white kids who I didn't have nothing in common with?" Kahila said with a sour taste. "Just because you and mom were the damn Jeffersons moving up in the world didn't mean that you had to send me away like I was some prisoner you were sending away to some remote island. Kids have feelings, too, you know."

"I realize that," Joshua said in angst. "And I realize that you may have been rebelling against me later on in your teenage years for shoving you away to boarding school. And I also realize that I may have contributed somewhat to your unfortunate long run with the law. I guess I'll take the blame for that."

The conversation between the two of them suddenly went dead silent.

"So I guess what I'm saying is that maybe now we can have the type of relationship with one another that we missed having together all those years before," Joshua said in an easy voice. "Maybe we can start all over and have the type of father and son relationship that we should've had a long time ago."

"I'm not a little kid anymore, daddy dearest," he said in a rough tone.

"No, you're certainly not, son," Joshua said in an easy voice. "But it's never too late to try, now is it?"

A long silence soon enveloped the car ride once again. The two countries were still not ready to resolve their deep rooted problems. The great Berlin Wall was still intact.

"Yeah . . ." Kahila finally uttered five minutes later as he continued to stare out of his passenger window. "What the hell."

Not another word was spoken, and certainly nothing more was going to be added. Kahila continued to stare out his passenger window like a statue as if determined not to turn and look at his father to show him any sort of tenderhearted kindness.

When Joshua finally arrived at Kahila's apartment complex, the two of them sat parked inside Joshua's car as if neither knew what to say or do next.

"Well, do you want me to walk you up to your apartment?"

Kahila suddenly busted out laughing. "Please, Pop, I'm not a little girl."

"Well, will I see you Sunday for dinner?"

"Sure, Pops, anything you say."

When Kahila got out of the car and headed for his apartment unit, Joshua took off and began to chuckle. A mile later, he couldn't help but laugh outright. Soon he simply couldn't control his hysterical outburst when he suddenly realized how ridiculous his words must've sounded when he asked his twenty-three-year-old, six-foot-three two hundred forty pound son if he needed an escort to his apartment.

Chapter 24

Joshua woke up at the crack of dawn the next morning. With hardly three hours of sleep after dealing with bailing Kahila out of jail and taking him home, Joshua had to head out once again. He had to take his wife to the airport so she could catch her eight a.m. flight to New York to attend her four day A Hand In Need annual national conference.

After fighting the busy L.A. morning traffic and finally returning home, Joshua climbed his staircase and went straight to bed for some much needed rest. He didn't care how long he slept. If he slept the entire day, it would suit him just fine. As tired as he was, he didn't care if he slept the entire week while Faye was away.

Six hours later, after getting some well-deserved sleep, Joshua finally woke up refreshed and well rested. Feeling rejuvenated, he figured he'd go for a light jog, then come back home and fix himself a nice lunch. After that, maybe he'd even get himself a few more hours of sleep. The thought of sleeping his day away sounded better and better the more he thought about it.

While putting on his running gear, Joshua suddenly grabbed the remote from the nightstand next to the bed and turned on the TV. When the TV came on, the breaking news report flashing across the screen nearly made him collapse to the floor with a massive heartache. Joshua literally couldn't believe the news report. In bold words it read: Ten Women From The Organization A Hand In Need Kidnapped In New York By Purification Of America Today!

Joshua literally began to shake as he stared at the TV screen. His insides began to swirl and tumble the longer he stared at the breaking news report. He literally couldn't breathe. The utter shock of the moment had taken his air and was suffocating him.

Suddenly his cellphone on the nightstand began to ring. With his heart beating in his throat, Joshua dashed to the nightstand and grabbed his cellphone. He immediately saw from the caller ID that it was Faye calling. A huge sigh of relief all of a sudden cascaded over his entire body. He began to breathe once again when he realized that Faye was calling to tell him that she was alright and safe.

"Hello, Faye," Joshua quickly answered, breathing heavily. "I just saw on the news what happened. I'm so glad you're okay."

"Oh, she's alright, *sweetheart*," the raspy old voice said with a snicker. "At least for now she is."

Joshua's heart literally stopped when he heard the sound of the voice. He was suddenly dead silent. He knew without a doubt who was on the phone.

"Did the cat suddenly snatch your tongue or are you that stunned to hear my voice?" the raspy old voice said when Joshua remained silent.

"Where's my wife?" Joshua finally muttered nervously.

"She's in our good care, Mr. Edwards, along with nine other women of her organization."

"Why are you doing this?"

"Why?" the voice said in a relaxed voice. "Well, Edwards, we didn't like what you did to us by leaving your blood brothers cold like that and taking those children along with you. That made us very angry."

"Please." His voice began to tremble. "You can't hurt her. You can't hurt my wife. Please!"

"Well, you'll just have to wait and see what happens to your wife, Edwards. We believe in an eye for an eye and a tooth for a tooth, and you just committed the ultimate sin by leaving us like you did. So there's a heavy price to pay for that. A *very* heavy price to pay," Kramer suddenly said in a sinister, cold voice. "Oh, and by the way, we took care of that other traitor also. Your good friend, Mr. Z, is no longer a brother of ours. We blew his brains out and scattered his worthless body to the wind in fifty different directions. That's how we paid back that miserable nigger lover!"

The call suddenly ended as Joshua held the phone limply in his hand. Even after the line went dead, he could still hear those chilling words echoing in his head.

Chapter 25

Joshua caught the first flight out of Los Angeles heading to New York. On the plane ride, he was more upset and more frightened than when he, himself, was kidnapped by Purification Of America Today. He knew full well what this sick, twisted organization was capable of. They were ruthless in their ambitions, and they would kill anybody to achieve their goals and the ideology that they tried to attain. There was no doubt Faye's life was in serious jeopardy; the members of Purification Of America Today were the sickest forms of human life that Joshua had ever encountered.

When Joshua's plane finally arrived at New York's LaGuardia Airport and he began to rush frantically through the busy airport to catch a cab, he was suddenly stopped by a horde of FBI agents inside the airport. Joshua was totally stunned to see so many FBI agents in front of him all of a sudden. They were like a road block that he hadn't expected.

The entire time since Joshua had left L.A., his mind had been focused on nothing but trying to locate his wife. It hadn't occurred to him while he was flying through the air, just how he would go about trying to locate where Purification Of America Today was hiding so he could find and rescue his wife. The only thing he knew was that his wife was in serious trouble and he had to do whatever he could to find her.

"Mr. Edwards," one of the agents quickly spoke as they all flashed their badges at him. "We're with the FBI and we were instructed by our superiors to stop you inside the airport when you arrived here in New York."

"How the hell did you know I was coming to New York?" Joshua said, glaring at the agents.

"We've been monitoring your movements and all of your communications since returning to Los Angeles after you escaped from Purification Of America Today with those kids. We didn't want to intrude totally in your life, but we had to keep an eye on you and try to protect you from further harm."

"So you've been tapping into my new cellphone, huh?"

"Your new cellphone, your house phone, and also your wife's cellphone."

"That's criminal invasion of my privacy!"

"Mr. Edwards, it's been for your safety," the agent said in an unapologetic voice. "We've had to use all angles possible to try to apprehend the rest of the members Purification Of America Today's organization and try to keep you and your wife safe. Unfortunately, your wife and nine other members of your wife's organization have been kidnapped by Purification Of America Today."

Joshua began to let his anger subside concerning the invasion of his privacy. At the moment, his wife's safety was all that mattered. "Look, I have to locate my wife," he said in a harried voice. "I don't have time for a million questions. So you gentlemen are going to have to excuse me."

"Mr. Edwards, that's what we've come to tell you. We've already located where Purification Of America Today is currently at. We've tracked them down and have them cornered. They're currently held up in a black bus in the middle of Times Square with your wife and the other nine hostages."

"In the middle of Times Square?" Joshua said as his eyes went wide with fear.

"Yes."

"Well, I have to go there immediately," he said in a panic. "I have to rescue my wife from those crazy lunatics."

"Mr. Edwards, the FBI has the situation well under control. We have the area totally corralled off and the black bus under constant surveillance with police and over a hundred of our agents right now on the location. We have the bus totally trapped in the middle of Times Square, Mr. Edwards, but there's a standoff currently going on. Purification Of America Today isn't releasing any of the hostages, and we're trying to bring the situation to a peaceful end."

"A standoff?"

"Yes, sir."

"You're going to have to take me down there at once." Joshua demanded as he glared at the agents standing in front of him. "Those lunatics have got my wife on that damn bus, and I can't just stand around here knowing she's in trouble."

"Mr. Edwards, we've been instructed to prevent that. The situation in Times Square is too dangerous. You're just going to have to let us take care of this problem. We'll do everything possible to bring the situation to a peaceful ending."

"No, I have to be down there right now," he said adamantly. "Out of my way, I'm catching a cab."

"A cab won't get you down there, Mr. Edwards. Times Square is totally blocked off."

"Then I'll find another way to get there."

"Mr. Edwards—"

"I must get down there at once!" Joshua suddenly yelled at the top of his lungs. People passing by in the busy airport began to stop and stare. "Those lunatics have my wife on that bus and I must be there with her. I must! Can't you understand? I must be there with her!"

The FBI agents all silently looked at one another as if to try to surmise the thoughts of each of their comrades. Finally the lead agent whipped out his cellphone and put in a call. After several minutes of chatting with someone, he hung up and looked firmly at Joshua.

"Alright, Mr. Edwards, come with us."

"Where are we going?"

"Times Square."

Times Square was literally a freak show. Thousands of people were packed everywhere to see what was going on. It was like New Year's Eve and the ball was getting ready to drop, but only there was no ball to drop; there was only a lone black bus in the middle of 42nd Street and Broadway in front of the famed One Times Square tower, and it contained the members of Purification Of America Today.

A myriad of police officers, FBI agents, and a plethora of SWAT team members desperately tried to keep the large, growing crowd in Times Square safely back from the lone black bus that was literally being quarantined. The standoff with the members of Purification Of America Today had now entered its eighth hour. Negotiations were simply going nowhere.

The FBI demanded the release of the hostages, but the members of Purification Of America Today continued to balk. They repeatedly threatened that if they weren't allowed to leave, they were going to kill all of the hostages. The FBI, after hearing this constant threat, would only continue to negotiate with their hostile nemeses on the black bus and try to keep them calm.

Joshua was worried sick. Despite being a civilian, the FBI had amazingly decided to allow him access into their inner circle. Joshua could hear the ongoing communications at the onsite command post that the FBI had set up as they tried to negotiate with the kidnappers on the black bus.

The conversation on the walkie-talkie radios and the speaker phone of the large radio was literally painful and excruciating to hear. The thought of his wife being held at gunpoint on that bus tore at his soul much worse than a bear claw ripping into his flesh. Each threat that Purification Of America Today made that they were about to kill all of the hostages, made his blood run colder than the North Pole. Whenever Joshua heard that, he literally wanted to run over to the quarantined black bus, pry open the doors of the bus, and rescue his wife from the agony that he knew she was going through.

In some ways, being allowed access into the inner circle of the FBI's negotiations was far worse than being one of the regular bystanders on the street of Times Square. Joshua knew if he were just a regular bystander, at least he wouldn't have to hear the screams and pleas of mercy from the women aboard the black bus whenever one of the members of Purification Of America Today threatened to kill them.

When midnight rolled around, the tense standoff had entered its twelfth hour. The crowd packed around Times Square had swelled to incredible proportions as more and more onlookers clamored to see what was going on. Every major news network was on the scene covering the harrowing event live to millions of viewers. The tense ongoing negotiations between Purification Of America Today and the FBI had become one of the longest standoffs ever. It quickly turned into a marathon to see which side could outlast the other.

Finally, a little after two a.m., Purification Of America Today was the first to blink. They said that they were ready to make a concession.

"Okay, what is your demand?" the FBI negotiator said into a walkie-talkie at the onsite command post when the leader of Purification Of America Today contacted him.

"We're ready to release the hostages if you do exactly as we say," Joshua heard the raspy voice of Bob Kramer come over the radio speaker at the command post.

"Okay, and what would that require on our part?"

"We're tired of lazy niggers pilfering money away from hard working taxpayers, gays corrupting our culture, wetback spics hording in and taking over this country, Muslims staining the red, white, and blue of our sacred flag, and a whole host of other despicable elements that are ruining this country," he said in an unwavering voice. "Because of this, we want a statement to flash across the advertising video screens of the One Times Square tower above us and across every news ticker of every building in Times Square to show the world how we, Purification Of America Today, feel about what's destroying this country. After each one of our statements is flashed across the video screens, we'll release a hostage."

"We have no control over these billboards and all the advertisement video screens you see here in Times Square," the FBI negotiator responded into the walkie-talkie. "That's an impossible request."

"You're the FBI," Kramer said with a nasty snarl in his voice. "See to it that it gets done, because that's the only way we're going to release these women that we have on this bus."

A long silence followed. All the FBI agents at the onsite command post suddenly looked at one another. A great debate quickly ensued as all the agents began to discuss the proposition set before them. Joshua looked on intensely and wondered would the FBI give in to such an unorthodox demand. The long standoff began to go deep into the night, and he was pretty sure at this late hour, anything was probably on the table.

Finally the lead FBI negotiator once again picked up the walkie-talkie.

"You'll have to give us time to see if we can get clearance to do something like that," he said into the walkie-talkie.

"We have all the time in the world, sir," Kramer said with his response. "You have us trapped in the middle of Times Square with thousands of people all around us. So we're not going anywhere."

A flood of calls were put in all over the place. From New York, Chicago, to Washington D.C., the FBI began to go up the chain of command trying to see what could be arranged. The task was daunting in its nature to try to achieve. It was literally overwhelming. It certainly wasn't easy trying to take one of the most valuable advertising locations in the world off the market so it could be used solely for propaganda that Purification Of America Today wanted to promote to the world.

Two hours later, the FBI had gotten the clearance that it needed. It was four a.m. when the lead FBI negotiator finally picked up the walkie-talkie once again.

"Alright, we have the clearance to do what you asked," he said into the walkie-talkie. "Now what?"

"We have our list of the nine things that we want put up on the video screens and news tickers on the Times Square buildings above us," Kramer's voice came through over the radio speaker at the onsite command post. "After each one is scrolled across the video screens and news tickers, we'll release a hostage to you."

"Are you able to send an email or a text message from that bus?"

"Yes."

"Alright, then send your list to this command site email in which we've setup. The email site is fbi/negotiations@nyc."

A minute later, the list of the nine things popped up on the large computer screen at the onsite command post. When all the FBI agents got a look at the nine messages to be displayed, they all glanced at one another in total silence.

The messages were some of the most appalling, racist rhetoric ever heard. Joshua desperately wanted his wife freed, but when he saw what Purification Of America Today wanted displayed on all the prominent video screens in Times Square, he truly wondered would the FBI actually put out such vain, despicable messages for the world to see.

"Look, we can't put those messages that you've sent us on any of the video screens or new tickers in Times Square," the lead FBI negotiator said into the walkie-talkie. "They're too insensitive."

"Oh, you'll put them out," Kramer said defiantly. "You'll do exactly as we say."

"But we've got news agencies from everywhere that's camped out here in Times Square," the FBI negotiator said. "The entire world is virtually watching."

"That's our whole point. We want the whole world to see what Purification Of America Today stands for."

"But we can't—"

"Put the damn messages out!" Kramer suddenly shouted across the radio speaker. "Because if you don't, in the next minute we're going to start throwing dead bodies off this damn bus!"

When the screams of the women on the bus suddenly came blaring once again over the radio speaker at the onsite command post when their lives were threatened, Joshua's stomach began to turn flips. His stomach had been going through a hellish agony for nearly twenty-four straight hours, and it had yet to stop torturing him. He knew the pain and discomfort was bound to get worse as the seconds and minutes of this ongoing nightmare slowly continued.

Finally the lead FBI negotiator, after hesitating for a long minute, turned and looked at the computer engineering specialist. He was brought in to operate the highly advanced system that controlled the video screens on the buildings in Times Square. The FBI negotiator, after procrastinating another long minute, slowly nodded his approval for the computer engineering specialist to go ahead and begin.

The messages began to go across the huge video screens and news tickers of the One Times Square skyscraper building and the other buildings in Times Square in successive fashion. One message would be released, then after a couple of minutes, another message would follow. All the major network news cameramen and reporters there on the scene began to capture the unprecedented moment. Thousands of onlookers packed inside Times Square watched as the messages scrawled across the video screens.

Gays And Fags Are No Longer Allowed In The USA

All Niggers Will Be Shipped Back To The Jungles Of Africa

The Jews Will Soon Meet A New Holocaust

All Muslims Leave The Country Immediately

Gun Control Proponents Will Be Put To Death By Firing Squad

All Illegal Mexican Immigrant Women Must Be Sterilized

Racial Profiling Will Become The Law Of The Land

The White Man Is The Only Man Who Will Lead America

Purification Of America Today Will Get A National Holiday

After each highly controversial message was released onto the video screens and news tickers of the One Times Square skyscraper building, a huge shocked gasp would erupt from the packed throng of people watching on the street. Just as Purification Of America Today had promised, though, a hostage was promptly released from the black bus after each message was displayed for the world to see. A horde of FBI agents would rush over to the hostage who'd just been released and quickly whisk the distraught woman away from the scene. Medical staff, waiting to provide the newly released hostage with care and comfort, would quickly take over from there.

With nine women released from the black bus and out of harm's away, only one hostage remained, Joshua's wife. The FBI waited patiently for Purification Of America Today to release the last hostage from the bus, but when fifteen minutes passed and she wasn't released, deep concern and trepidation began to form on all the faces of the agents.

"There's still one hostage aboard the bus," the FBI negotiator finally spoke into his walkie-talkie. "That hostage must be released."

"Well, we've certainly kept our word and have given you nine of our hostages," the voice of Kramer came across the radio at the onsite command post. "We've kept our word, haven't we?"

"No, you haven't," the negotiator said as he snapped. "There were ten hostages aboard that bus and all ten hostages must be released."

"Well, you are correct," Kramer's voice said when it came across the radio. "We're still holding one hostage aboard our bus, and that would be Mrs. Joshua Edwards."

"And that hostage must be released, also."

"Well, Mrs. Edwards is going to require something of a far more significant statement to the world before she can be released," Kramer's voice said when it came across the radio.

Joshua listened intently to the radio with his heart pounding like an earthquake registering a 10.0. His stomach was now literally doing summersaults and back flips faster than an Olympic gymnast.

"What further statement do you want?"

"In order for Mrs. Joshua Edwards to be freed from this bus, we, Purification Of America Today, require the release of Mr. Dylan Roof from the South Carolina detention center that he's currently being held in."

All the FBI agents stared at one another in muted silence. Joshua slowly clutched his chest and stomach as if a heartache and an ulcer had suddenly besieged him all at once.

"That's impossible," the FBI negotiator finally said into the walkie-talkie after the long silence. "It can't be done."

"If Dylan Roof isn't released in exactly one hour, then Mrs. Edwards is going to die," Kramer said in a haunting voice.

"That's crazy. There's no possible way to—"

"One hour or she dies!" his voice whipped across the radio. "You got one hour!"

When the leader of Purification Of America Today made the last demand for the release of Dylan Roof, all the agents quickly began to formulate another plan to try to get the last hostage released. There were no urgent phone calls to any of the higher ups in Washington or anywhere else concerning the demand they'd just received. The demand was so outrageous and unattainable that there was no need to even put an effort to try to make it happen.

Furthermore, the demand was downright insane. It was an insane demand that indicated that this evil organization was hell-bent on killing the last remaining hostage no matter what. If the FBI didn't come up with something to try to stop this ruthless organization, an unspeakable horror was about to occur for everyone in Times Square and the entire world to witness.

While the FBI worked feverishly to come up with an alternate plan to get the last hostage released, Joshua was about to literally go out of his mind. The petrified fear that had taken over his body was so severe that he couldn't stop shaking.

The thought of Faye sitting alone on that black bus thirty feet from him, and the thought of the terror she was going through at this very moment, made Joshua cringe like never before. He desperately wanted to change places with his wife and be the one sitting on that bus being terrorized by those lunatics whom he'd come to know so well over the last couple of weeks. If death was going to come, he'd much prefer it would be him who faced it. At least he'd know that his wife would be the one who was safe and sound at the FBI command post, and he could go ahead and die in total peace.

Finally an hour later when dawn began to break over the Manhattan skyline, Kramer's voice came across the FBI radio command post once again.

"An hour has now passed," the old raspy voice said. "Has Mr. Dylan Roof been freed from the South Carolina detention center?"

Joshua desperately hoped the FBI would lie so that it would maybe appease the whims of Purification Of America Today.

"No, he hasn't," the FBI negotiator answered. "We can't assist in making that request happen."

Soon as the FBI negotiator gave his answer, the door to the black bus suddenly opened. The last hostage was shoved out of the bus as the doors quickly closed. Faye began to take about ten steps away from the bus when all of a sudden she collapsed to ground yelling and crying out in agony. All the FBI agents began to rush over to aid her, but they quickly stopped in their tracks and began to retreat.

Faye, looking like a suicide bomber, was strapped and locked into a sophisticated bomb vest. The bomb vest was packed with all sorts of explosives as a digital clock attached to the vest ticked down with only twenty seconds left.

Joshua, like an enraged bull, immediately began to charge straight for his wife, who was lying helplessly in the middle of the road yelling and crying. Five FBI agents quickly seized Joshua and forcefully restrained him from getting any closer. The sheer agony of seeing his wife lying in the middle of the road, with only seconds from exploding, was as torturous as a razor sharp knife cutting straight through his soul.

The seconds on the digital clock ticked fast. Ten seconds, nine seconds, eight seconds; everyone packed in Times Square literally held their breath as they watched the agony unfold. Seven seconds, six seconds, five seconds; Joshua fought and scratched with all of his might to get to his wife as the FBI agents still restrained him. Four seconds, three seconds, two seconds; Faye closed her eyes as she appeared to prepare to die. One second; everyone had moved back as far as they could.

When the digital clock on the bomb vest struck zero, absolutely nothing happened, then, without notice or warning, the black bus ten feet from Faye suddenly exploded. It erupted into a hellish ball of fire forty feet into the air as debris from the bus flew and landed everywhere.

Chaos was rampant. As FBI agents and SWAT team members scattered frantically trying to keep the hellish situation under control and thousands of onlookers watched in horror at what had transpired, Joshua quickly went to the aide of his wife lying helpless in the street. The dazed, shocked look on her face was that of a ghost who had just seen death, but still lived to experience the horror of it all.

Joshua, with great care, slowly reached down and helped his wife up from the street. With the bomb vest, which was apparently nothing but an elaborate ruse, still strapped around her like a restraining jacket, Faye collapsed into her husband's arms and cried like never before.

As Joshua held his shell-shocked grieving wife tightly in his arms, he stared at the burning wreckage that was once the black bus that had held the ten ladies of A Hand In Need hostage for nearly twenty straight hours. It was devastating and also exhilarating to see the wreckage burning so profusely as the sun steadily rose over the sky.

On the one hand, it was exhilarating to know that the organization that had caused so much harm and misery to so many people couldn't harm anybody any longer, but on the other hand, it was also devastating because Purification Of America Today had gone out completely on their own terms. They wouldn't have to face the justice and punishment that they so richly deserved; instead, they had decided their own fate. With their backs against the wall and nowhere to run, in front of the entire world, these evil, twisted renegades decided to take one final suicide mission and go out in a blaze of glory.

Chapter 26

All ten rescued hostages were taken to the nearest hospital in Manhattan for counseling, therapy, and further evaluation. Most of it was for precautionary reasons. After dealing with such a tremendous, stressful ordeal being held hostage for nearly twenty hours and facing constant death, the authorities weren't taking any chances. The mental and physical state of each rescued hostage was the FBI's top concern.

Faye was in a private hospital room resting comfortably in a hospital bed while Joshua stood by her bedside giving her all the support and love that she needed. A policeman was stationed outside her hospital room, not to prevent anyone from entering her room to do her harm, but to prevent the horde of reporters loitering around her hospital room from barging in.

Dozens of reporters desperately sought an opportunity to get an interview from Faye. Being the last hostage freed from that black bus by Purification Of America Today made her somewhat of the star hostage whom all the reporters wanted to interview. Plus, the dramatic way in which the long standoff finally ended with her almost being blown to bits, even though the bomb vest she wore was nothing but a ruse, still made her the number one subject the reporters clamored to see.

Joshua gently caressed Faye's hair while he stood beside her hospital bed. He looked down at her with deep compassion as Faye watched the overhead TV in the room. The TV was on the news, and they were talking nonstop about the hostage incident that took place at Times Square.

"You want me to turn off the TV?" Joshua said with compassion. "I know that's the last thing you want to relive."

"How about turning the channel to some comedy or something?" Faye said, gazing up at Joshua. "I could use a little laughter in my life."

Joshua grabbed the remote control connected to the bed and began to flip through the channels.

"Oh, there's *The Jeffersons*," he said with a wondrous smile. "I know how you used to always love watching George and Weezie."

"That's fine," she suddenly said with a soft chuckle.

Joshua and Faye began to slowly hold hands as they looked into each other's eyes. The stone silence between them, while they stared into each other's eyes, began to go on for quite a while. It was like a soothing, healing remedy that they both seemed to need at the moment.

"Why did this have to happen to us, Joshua?" Faye finally said in a dreary voice. "Why did this have to happen at all?"

"I don't know," he said, slowly shaking his head. "I guess you'll have to ask Purification Of America Today that question."

"I can't. They're no longer around."

"Thank the Lord for that."

"Joshua, when they forced me into that vest with all those explosives and shoved me out of that bus with that clock ticking, I thought I only had seconds to live," she said with her eyes swelling with tears. "I thought it was all over. I literally saw my life flash before my eyes."

"Try not to focus on that," he said when he slowly squeezed her hand. "You're here now and that's all that matters."

"Am I really?" she said in a dismal voice. "I don't know how long it's going to take me to get over this, if I ever will."

"We got all the time in the world," Joshua said in a caring voice. He wiped away the tears that began to stream down her face. "There's no hurry."

"It might take weeks."

"We have a lot of weeks ahead of us."

"It may take months."

"We've got loads of months."

"It may even take years."

"We have *plenty* of years in front of us," Joshua said with a chuckle. "And plenty more years after that."

"I guess you're right," she said as her tears began to subside.

"Aren't I always right?"

"No," she said, suddenly breaking into a little smile. "That's why you need me around, to make your wrongs right."

"You bet I do," Joshua said. He kneeled and gave her a soft kiss on the lips. "I'm going to step out for a while and let you get some rest now. I'll be back shortly and check on you."

Faye nodded and gave a slight smile once again.

Joshua watched as she slowly closed her eyes. When she finally drifted off to sleep, he left her bedside and eased out of the hospital room. The police officer was still sitting by the room's door side as a couple of reporters, who'd been loitering around, immediately besieged Joshua wanting a quick interview. He quickly waved them off and headed down the hall toward the elevator.

When Joshua reached the elevator, two FBI agents, whom he recognized as part of the FBI negotiating team assigned to the onsite command post at Times Square, were coming off the elevator. The three of them immediately struck up a conversation.

"How's your wife, Mr. Edwards?"

"She's going to be fine," Joshua said in a confident voice. "She just needs a lot of rest."

"You're leaving?"

"I'm just going down to the cafeteria for a bite to eat," he said. "How's the investigation wrapping up? What's the conclusion to the story of that bus exploding like it did?"

"It looks like Purification Of America Today was totally prepared to go out at a moment's notice. From all the evidence that we've been collecting at the site of the explosion in Times Square, it looks like they had enough explosives stored on that bus to blow the bus four times over if necessary."

"And these were very high level grades of explosives, too," the other agent said. "We're fortunate that no one else was hurt with so many people packed around that area."

"What about the bomb vest that was strapped around my wife? I was told that it was nothing but a contrived decoy, correct?"

"No, that bomb vest was *very* real."

"But we were told at the site that it was just a ruse."

"On our first inspection of that vest, on all levels, it appeared to be nothing but a phony contraption. But when our bomb experts took it apart, they discovered that it was a highly sophisticated bomb vest packed with real explosives, much like what exploded the bus."

"But the digital clock attached to the bomb vest went all the way down to zero and nothing happened," Joshua said as he looked at the agents suspiciously. "And even after that bus exploded, my wife was still locked in that vest for nearly half an hour before your bomb unit was able to take it off."

"After a further, deeper inspection of that device, we discovered that particular sophisticated bomb vest could only be triggered by a remote apparatus that someone controls. The time ticking down from that digital clock connected to the vest had no correlation to it actually exploding."

"You mean the entire time she was in that thing, someone on that bus could've actually triggered the bomb vest and exploded it?"

The agents nodded gravely. "Consider your wife fortunate to still be around, Mr. Edwards."

Joshua suddenly felt his stomach begin to toss and turn like a violent hurricane was inside it. His legs became so wobbly and weak that he thought he was about to collapse.

"And one further thing," one of the agents said. He suddenly handed Joshua a wadded piece of paper. "We found this deep inside the vest among the explosives. I think you might want to read it."

When the agents headed down the hospital hall, Joshua got into the elevator and punched for the fifth floor where the cafeteria was located. As the elevator began to slowly descend, Joshua unfolded the piece of paper that the FBI agents handed him. He slowly began to read what it contained:

Dear Edwards:

It is only because you were once a blood brother of our esteemed organization that we've decided to spare your wife the agony of being blown away. You can thank us for our generosity when we meet on the other side. But if we decide to change our minds and blow the bitch away to kingdom come at the very last second, then you'll know that you were the reason for her tragic death. A blood brother never does what you did by running out on his brothers. You are a disgrace to ever be called a member of Purification Of America Today!

Bob Kramer

When the elevator finally stopped on the fifth floor and the doors opened, Joshua was so stunned and rattled at what he'd just read that he couldn't move even the slightest inch. With no movement, the doors eventually closed as the elevator proceeded on to another floor.

Chapter 27

Three days later, Faye was finally about to be released from the hospital. The doctors had determined that she was able to proceed with her life and continue being a productive citizen of society. Healing her mental wounds would still take some time, but her journey of life could continue uninhibited.

When the doctors gave the wonderful news of his wife's soon release, Joshua decided to get out of the hospital for a while and take in a couple of sights of New York. After visiting some of New York's iconic historical sites, Joshua ended his tour of the Big Apple by taking a ferry cruise to Liberty Island from Manhattan to get a look at the Statue of Liberty.

After spending an hour and a half viewing the fabulous, magnificent structure of the Statue of Liberty up close, Joshua had a seat on one of the park benches near the statue as he began to take in what this great American symbol meant. Seeing the illustrious statue up close and personal suddenly made him think about Purification Of America Today.

Joshua remembered when he first visited Purification Of America Today's website. He recalled how they claimed that they wanted to purify America of all of its undesirable elements and how they wanted to ignite a fire in young zealots all over the nation to take up their cause and complete their so-called holy mission. However, seeing the Statue of Liberty gleaming in the brilliant sunlight began to ignite in Joshua a different kind of passion of what America stood for. That passion burned inside him like the flame that the Lady of Liberty held, and he was burning to tell the entire world.

Joshua pulled out his laptop that he carried with him, and as he sat on that bench staring in wonder at the great sight before him, he logged onto his computer and went straight to his blog, Justice For All. The last entry he'd made was forced upon him by Purification Of America Today, but today as he stared at the beauty of the Statue of Liberty before him, the words he was about to tell the world would be all his own.

Titling his new blog entry The Torch Of Freedom, Joshua began to type his new blog:

The Torch Of Freedom

America is a special, unique country; there's not one like it in the entire world. It is comprised of many different varieties of people, ethnicities, colors, and languages all rolled together to form one nation and one union. It is a nation of promise and of opportunity where the torch of freedom shines brightly for everyone to constantly see and will never be extinguished.

Purification Of America Today tried in vain to extinguish the great torch of freedom, but the flame of freedom still burns brighter than ever. They wanted to ignite a fire in young zealots like them to continue their efforts to start a war against what America stands for, and that's justice and equality for all. Blacks, Muslims, Hispanics, homosexuals, Jews, liberals, and many others became their targets of hate in their quest to make America a one state of non-diversity. They wanted to purify the blood that ran through America whom they deemed unfit to enjoy the torch of freedom that burns ever brightly, but their misguided efforts of hate and cruelty in the end merely flamed out, unlike the torch of freedom that blazes on.

Unfortunately, there will be others who will come along, other groups of evil and malcontent who will try to extinguish the great torch of freedom that burns so brightly for everyone to see; however, we must all stand together and combat this type of an invasion on our freedom. The great torch that is lit must stay ablaze and never be extinguished.

When Joshua finished his entry into his blog, he sent it off and once again gazed at the Statue of Liberty. Finally, he put away his laptop and rose from the bench and glanced at his watch. He saw that it was 3 p.m., and it was nearing that time for his wife to be released from the hospital.

More important, Joshua knew it was nearing the time for he and his wife to continue that journey together down that long road of life. He'd promised her by the hospital bed that they had plenty of years of happiness left together, and he hoped and prayed that he was correct. With a tremendous joy suddenly filling his entire heart, he began to smile as he headed to catch the ferry ride back to Manhattan.

To Read Other Suspense Novels By Vincent Armstrong log onto:

www.vincentarmstrong.com

For Comments Contact The Author At:

vincentarmstrong@bellsouth.net

www.ingramcontent.com/pod-product-compliance
Lightning Source LLC
Chambersburg PA
CBHW050929120626
46552CB00001B/113